ROGUE

ROGUE

HER PARANORMAL MAJESTY'S SECRET SERVICE™
BOOK 01

MICHAEL ANDERLE

THE ROGUE TEAM

Thanks to the Beta Readers
James Caplan, Larry Omans, John Ashmore, Kelly O'Donnell,
Mary Morris

Thanks to the JIT Readers
Dave Hicks
Deb Mader
Debi Sateren
Dorothy Lloyd
Jackey Hankard-Brodie
Jeff Eaton
Jeff Goode
Larry Omans
Lori Hendricks
Micky Cocker
Paul Westman
Peter Manis

If I've missed anyone, please let me know!

Editor
The Skyhunter Editing Team

LMBPN Publishing
PMB 196, 2540 South Maryland Pkwy
Las Vegas, NV 89109

First US Edition, December 2020
(Previously published as a part of *Rogue, Renegade & Rebel*)
Version 1.01, December 2020
ebook ISBN: 978-1-64971-364-3
Print ISBN: 978-1-64971-365-0

DEDICATION

*To Family, Friends and
Those Who Love
to Read.
May We All Enjoy Grace
to Live the Life We Are
Called.*

— Michael

GENEVIEVE KING'S
UK TO US TRAVEL GUIDE

An insight into how the Americans butcher the queen's English

UK (Correct) — *US (Wrong)*

- **Aluminium (*ah-luh-min-ee-um*)** — Aluminum (*ah-loo-min-uhm…WHAT?*)
- **American Football** — *Football*
- **Bathroom / Toilet / Loo** — *Restroom*
- **Biscuit** — *Cookie*
- **Bonnet (Car)** — *Hood*
- **Broadsheet** — *Newspaper*
- **Car Park** — *Parking Lot*
- **Chips** — *French Fries*
- **Crisps** — *Potato Chips*
- **Dual carriageway** — *Highway, freeway*
- **Dummy** — *Pacifier*
- **Duvet** — *Blanket (yes there are duvets, but not in this story)*
- **Extension lead** — *Extension cord*
- **Flat** — *Apartment*
- **Football** — *Soccer*
- **Garden** — *Yard*
- **Holiday** — *Vacation*
- **Ice lolly** — *Popsicle*
- **Jumper** — *Sweater*
- **Knickers** — *Panties*
- **Lift** — *Elevator*
- **Lorry** — *Truck*
- **Mad** — *Insane / Crazy*
- **Motorway** — *Highway*
- **Mummy** — *Mommy*

- **Nappy** — *Diaper*

- **Number Plate** — *License Plate*

- **Oregano (*or-i-gah-no*)** — *Oregano (or-eh-ga-no...I mean, come on!)*

- **Pants** — *Underwear*

- **Pavement** — *Sidewalk*

- **Peckish** — *Hungry*

- **Police / Bobbies / Pigs / Boys in Blue** — *Cops / Police*

- **Potato (*poh-tah-to*)** — *Potato (pah-tay-to)*

- **Rubbish** — *Trash*

- **Shop** — *Store*

- **Sofa** — *Couch*

- **Sweets** — *Candy*

- **Torch** — *Flashlight*

- **Tomato (*toh-mah-to*)** — *Tomato (tah-may-to)*

- **Trainers** — *Sneakers*

- **Trollied** — *Drunk/plastered*

- **Trousers** — *Pants*

- **Tube** — *Subway*

- **Waistcoat** — *Vest*

- **Wardrobe** — *Closet*

- **Windscreen** — *Windshield*

PROLOGUE

Brussels, Belgium, 1955

Vinnie Romano sat between the pair of hooded young women in the back of the black Jaguar. Its engine purred, the only sound since the sun had long gone to sleep and the moon was high in the sky.

A thin layer of mist floated along the ground. There was a chill in the air as Marco pulled onto the street and cut the engine.

Vinnie grunted. "This the place?"

"Of course." Marco clicked his tongue and exited the vehicle, revealing a small flash of the pistol holstered to his hip as the moon's light caught the body of the weapon.

"Fine." Vinnie opened the rear door and gave the first girl a shove, sending her out of the car and sprawling onto the ground. He laughed, grabbed the other's arm, and pulled her along with him, ignoring the muffled moans from beneath the hessian sack over her head.

Marco was busy helping the first girl to her feet. "Careful with the merchandise. They don't like them when they're bruised. It knocks the asking price."

What's a couple of hundred lire to the Messino brothers? Vinnie thought, but he held his tongue.

Marco led the way, strolling up to the front door of the rundown apartment complex. Five stories high, number eighty-two was the only building that showed any signs of life at this time of night. A faint flicker of candlelight shone from several of the windows above them.

The door opened, just an inch.

"Yo, Tony, it's Marco. We've got the boss' package. You gonna let us in, or are we gonna have to shout from the streets and wake the fucking neighbors?"

The door opened another fraction. A head the size of a beach-ball poked out, the face stony as a gargoyle. He examined the four figures standing on his doorstep, his eyes lingering a little too long on the white-stained dresses of the two girls, before grunting his approval and removing the latch.

Marco thanked Tony as he walked on by. Vinnie couldn't help but notice the gigantic gargoyle of a man lick his lips as they passed into the apartment and headed toward the stairs.

The air was smoky and stank of cigarettes. All along the corridor, there were men stationed, each resting with their back and the sole of a foot against the wall. Many wore white shirts, black suspenders striping their tops and their brows hidden by fedoras. All had a gun at their hip—a precautionary measure enforced by the brothers at the top.

Vinnie spotted filthy mattresses on the floors through several of the doorways they passed. Most of the rooms were a state, with stains on the floors, yellow wallpaper that curled like hang-nails, and empty bottles all over.

Vinnie's heart rate quickened. He was excited about this. Nervous, but excited. Being a lowly grunt in the whole operation, he had been surprised to have been selected as part of the force that would be sent out to ensure that the deed was done for the brothers.

This is your moment, Vinnie Boy. Time to make it big, earn that top cash, and show them what you're made of. Don't fuck it up.

They passed the third floor, then the fourth. They nodded return acknowledgments to members of the gang, although some ignored them entirely—jealousy, most likely. Everyone wanted a piece of the action that night—the clincher of the deal that had been months in the making.

When they reached the final flight of stairs, Vinnie was certain he could hear the grunts of people in the next room doing the dirty—*"making luuuurve,"* as his wife would say. He cocked an ear, a grin on his face, not paying attention as the girl in front of him slipped and fell forward.

She moaned as her face whacked the stairs.

"Fuck's sake, Vinnie, what did I tell you?" Marco pulled the girl to her feet. Her sobs were stifled by the material over her head, which had begun to blossom with blood.

"Oh, they're going to love this," Marco snapped. A nearby grunt sniggered. "And you can shut your fucking mouth, too." He squared up to the grunt. "Unless you want me to tell them that the little virgin they paid a pretty price for was actually deflowered in the car by a prospective member of their gang?"

The grunt instantly shut up, the color draining from his face.

"That's what I thought." Marco patted the girl down like a mother ironing out the creases to get her child ready for her first day at school. He took the hood off, revealing a disheveled young girl no older than seventeen, her face a mask of blood. Her dark hair clung to her sweaty forehead, and there was a terrified look on her face. "Keep still."

Marco produced a tissue from his pockets and cleaned her up, getting rid of as much of the blood as possible. He was gentle, cooing over the girl even though she hissed at the touch of the tissue on her nose. It stopped bleeding pretty quickly, which helped him a lot.

When he was done, he held her shoulders and took a good look. "There. Good as new."

He grinned.

She did not return the smile.

"Lucky for me, I've brought spares," Marco told Vinnie. He pulled out another hood, which he placed delicately over her head.

Vinnie grew impatient. "Can we go now?"

"Sure thing, pal." There was a hint of sarcasm in Marco's voice. "Maybe this time don't damage the goods, and we can get this done sometime before sunup. How about that?"

Vinnie's face grew red.

They knocked three times on the uppermost door, and a shout from the room gave them permission to enter. Marco grinned back at Vinnie and muttered, "Are you ready for the big leagues, worm?"

Vinnie simply swallowed and followed him inside.

Compared to the other rooms that he had passed, this one was actually hospitable.

There was a four-poster in the far corner. The furniture looked brand-new. Through the smoky haze of the brothers' cigarettes, he saw a number of comfortable plush chairs dotted around the room, two of which were occupied by the Messino Brothers.

Eugenio and Carmelo sat back in their chairs, cigars clamped between their teeth. They looked near enough identical with their crisp suits, hair slicked back, and their eyes fixed on the girls. They each sported the kind of chubbiness in their faces that came with the comforts of being well-provided for. The pair hardly needed more cash, but what was life if not for the pleasure of coin and sex?

Carmelo rose from his chair and stretched out his arms, walking over to Marco and embracing him. He placed a kiss on both his cheeks, then crossed to Vinnie.

"I knew you could do it, new blood." Carmelo's grin was broad. He turned back to his brother. "Didn't I tell you, Eugenio? Didn't I tell you I could see his potential?" He wrapped his arm around Vinnie's shoulder. "This one here, he's gonna go far, I tell you. He *delivers*."

"Show them to me," Eugenio ordered flatly, clearly not prepared to share his brother's enthusiasm until the deed was done.

Carmelo roughly grabbed Vinnie's cheeks and kissed the left, then right before sitting down again cheerfully. He crossed his legs and stared greedily at the girls.

Marco caught Vinnie's eye, took a breath, and ripped off the girls' hoods.

They were pretty, like china dolls plucked straight from a shelf and granted the same wish that had made Pinocchio a real boy. They were near-enough identical, with piercing blue eyes that stood out on their paper-white faces like sapphires on snow.

Carmelo clapped loudly. "Oh, bravo. Bravo."

Vinnie breathed a sigh of relief, his entire body softening. He had feared that the fall on the stairs would screw everything up and risk his chances of making it into the inner circle, but it looked like they hadn't—

"Wait." Eugenio's voice punctuated the room. His eyes narrowed as he peeled himself out of his seat and crossed to the pair. He scrutinized both girls through slitted eyes, his nostrils widening as he inhaled their scent. He ran a finger across their cheeks, and they shivered beneath his touch. He circled them, taking in every centimeter of their being before returning to the front once more.

Vinnie and Marco held their breath.

Eugenio leaned forward and touched his stubby, nicotine-stained fingers to the girl's nose. He withdrew and examined the small dark drop of blood on his fingertip. "What's this?"

His voice was deep, the low growl of a lion.

Vinnie looked at Marco for help. Marco rolled his eyes. "A minor hiccup, Eugenio. The girl is clumsy; she fell before we could catch her—"

Before he could finish, Eugenio lashed out and sent a large fist into his cheek.

Eugenio rocked on his heels, moved over to Vinnie, and delivered a similar blow with his left.

Pain exploded in Vinnie's mouth. He tasted copper and felt a tooth come free. His hand found his cheek, and he stayed crouched for fear of a second blow.

"Perfect condition," Eugenio uttered, his voice already level. "I asked for *perfect condition*. Do you know who these two are? They're the daughters of one of the wealthiest families in all of France. They'll fetch a price on the market that you could only dream of. Enough cash to make you go blind. You think I can risk this trade by having you break their nose and clot their nostrils with blood?"

Carmelo leaned forward, unfazed by his brother's reaction. "In all fairness, brother, her nose doesn't look broken."

Eugenio cocked his head and held the girl's cheeks in his hands. He stared at her for a long moment. "You're right," he said at last. "You're right. Still…" He pulled out his gun and aimed it at Vinnie's chest. "You only get one chance with the Messino brothers, and you fucked it up, new blood."

The report was loud, echoing around the apartment like a thunderclap. Vinnie's hands moved automatically to his chest, a girlish scream coming from his mouth as his eyes screwed shut. He waited for the pain to explode in his chest…

But no pain came.

He opened his eyes. Eugenio and Carmelo were now on their feet, alert and listening.

"What the fuck was that?" Eugenio asked. "I thought you said *all* our men were armed with silenced pistols?"

"They are," Carmelo replied, though he suddenly seemed uncertain. "Every one of them since the East Polar docks in '52."

For the first time since Vinnie had met him, Eugenio looked afraid. Another report came from below them, followed by ten more in quick succession. They heard raised voices, alarm spreading through the apartment like fire through a woodpile.

"Well, don't just stand there," Eugenio barked at Vinnie and Marco. "Go!"

Vinnie imagined he must have looked a sight to Eugenio as his mouth flapped open. His face betrayed his fear as Marco grabbed him by the shoulder and shoved him into the hallway.

Gunshots were coming from everywhere. The loud reports of the infiltrators' weapons were interrupted by the muted pops of the silenced Colts of the grunts in the corridors. Plaster dust had built up into a haze that stung their eyes as they ran down the stairs toward their fellow mobsters' cries.

"Get your ass in gear," Marco called from up ahead. There was a hungry look in his eyes, the look of someone who believed they could be the one—the single person to stop the rampage and claim the glory for his captain.

He disappeared around the corner of the stairwell. A moment later came the loudest shot yet, followed by blood splattering on the wall. Marco's lifeless body was thrown backward with a hole in his chest big enough to shake hands through.

All courage failed Vinnie. He scrambled backward and leaped up the stairs two at a time. He only made it to the next landing when he felt the bullets rip his insides and snuff out the light, the momentum enough to turn him and give him the briefest of glimpses of his attacker.

The most terrifying woman he had ever seen.

Eugenio heard the gunshots cease. The house fell into a heavy silence. He blinked nervously but puffed out his chest. Whatever was to come, he would handle it like a man. He had been through worse, dammit, and he had always come out on top.

Carmelo stood beside him. Both brothers had their weapons aimed at the open doorway. They could hear them—someone coming up the stairs. Their steps were light, but they were coming.

In the corner of the room, the girls huddled together, their hands bound and mouths gagged.

"The first sighting you get, take your shot," Eugenio side-mouthed.

"And if it's one of our own?"

"Fuck 'em. We can find new people."

Carmelo nodded, resolute.

The footsteps grew closer, and the sound got louder. To Eugenio, it sounded as if they were on the landing and now approached the room, although he couldn't see anyone. Maybe just the faintest shimmer, as though a heated air vent had opened and rippled the air.

"Eugenio?"

"Hey, reprobates," came a voice from next to them. "Mind if I join the party?"

Before the brothers could react, she fired and knocked the guns from their hands. They clattered impotently to the floor as their hands clapped to their ears.

"Who's there?" Eugenio shouted, the volume unnecessary in the quiet house. "Show yourself!"

"She's one of those. She's one of *those!*" Carmelo squealed, whirling in a panic as he looked for their attacker.

The woman materialized out of nowhere. "One of what?" She cocked her head to the side, a grin painted on her face. She wore round-framed glasses with tinted lenses. In one hand, she held a small pistol, and in the other, something that could easily have been a sawed-off shotgun but was nothing like any rifle the brothers had ever seen. Both weapons were aimed at the men's genitalia.

Carmelo's voice quivered. "She's a ghost. She's a fucking *ghost.*"

The woman walked toward the brothers, her hips swaying seductively as she did so. "Oh, you have me all wrong. I'm not a ghost, sweetheart. I'm not like anything you've ever seen before."

Eugenio scowled, eyes darting to his weapon on the floor. "Then who are you?"

The woman smiled. "I'm your worst fucking nightmare. I'm the bitch they send in to clean up the big messes, and oh, boy, have you two made a big mess!"

"You've got nothing on us," Eugenio muttered. "We're bulletproof—"

Eugenio stopped talking the second the bullets entered his body.

She fired from both guns, holes appearing on his body in a matter of seconds. The girls in the corner screamed and Carmelo fell to the floor with his hands over his head.

When she was finished, Eugenio's body hit the floor, the light gone from his eyes.

"He doesn't seem bulletproof to me." The woman sighed, then turned the gun on Carmelo. "How about you, handsome? Think you'd fare better than your brother?"

Carmelo shook with fear. "Please! Please, no. I beg of you. Don't hurt me!"

The woman turned to the girls in the corner. "See? All it takes is the simple threat of a gun, and men fall to their knees faster than they think *you* will for the right bidder." She turned her back on Carmelo and crossed the room, then knelt before the girls.

The sisters recoiled as she approached. "You don't need to worry anymore. We're getting you back to your parents. This nightmare is over." She wiped away their tears and gave them a reassuring smile. "You're both safe now. Trust me, I'll get you home."

The girls looked blankly at her. She couldn't misread the alarm on their faces, but she did what she could to assure them in their own language. *"Vous êtes tous les deux en sécurité maintenant. Croyez-moi. Je te ramène à la maison."*

Rough, but it did the job.

She untied their hands and pulled the gag from their mouths. As she was on the final knot, she heard movement from behind. The girls pointed, now that their hands were free.

But she was prepared.

Without looking, the woman aimed her pistol and pulled the trigger. A neat hole appeared in Carmelo's forehead. He fell to his knees, his pistol still clutched tightly in his hands.

"They never learn." The woman shook her head. "No matter how many chances you give them."

She helped the girls to their feet and told them to follow her in the same halting French. When she reached the door, she realized they were still in the corner, their feet glued to the floor.

One of the girls looked at the woman with wide eyes. When she spoke, it was with a thick French accent. "Who...Who are you?"

The woman took off her glasses and tucked them into her pocket. "I go by a lot of names, but you two can call me Rogue."

Sirens began to blare a few streets away. The police had been alerted to the shootout in the suburbs.

Rogue ushered the two girls onward, and they were gone before the first police officer kicked down the door.

CHAPTER ONE

<u>New York City, USA, Present Day</u>

"This isn't proper. You know you've come here to complete a task. What good is alcohol in helping you achieve your mission?"

Genevieve "Jennie" King raised the shot glass to her lip, sniffed the thick licorice tones of the liquid, and let it fall onto her tongue. The sambuca warmed every part of her it touched, the buzz making her come alive.

The man beside her, Worthington Conrad, clicked his tongue and turned away, folding his arms. He would have been an unusual sight at the New York bar, a vibrant little place by the elegant name of Shots, Shots, Shots. If his thick British accent hadn't marked him as a stranger to these lands, his clothing certainly would have given the game away.

If anyone could *see* him, of course.

"I'm not talking to you," Jennie told him, raising her hand to the bartender to indicate another round for herself. "You don't exist, remember?"

Worthington huffed. "You don't have to be so obtuse about it. If I didn't exist, could I do this?" He turned to the man on the stool beside him and sat on his lap, his entire body disappearing into the unlucky stranger's.

The man's eyes widened, and he choked on his cocktail. He shuddered and looked around for the source of the chill.

Jennie rolled her eyes. If there was one thing she hated about being permanently babysat by one of the queen's specters, it was their selfish need to feel valued.

Ego, ego, ego. That was all any of them cared about.

Worthington came out of the man's body and took his seat beside Jennie once again. "You were saying?"

Jennie was unimpressed. "Oh, great—you can make people feel cold. When will your powers cease to amaze? If only I could make people chilly, I could make a right killing moving closer to the equator and offering a human air conditioning service."

Worthington's face fell, and he turned his nose up. "Well, at least I don't need to find my happiness in the bottom of a bottle."

Jennie opened her mouth to speak, then saw the bartender approach and shut it quickly, knowing that no one else could see the pompous form of the former royal guard sitting next to her. She was used to the strange stares she got from others when she spoke to her specter. That didn't mean that she didn't occasionally fancy the night off from it.

"You know you look ridiculous, right?" Worthington commented. "I mean, who wears sunglasses indoors?"

Jennie shrugged. "They're a part of my look, okay?"

Worthington curled his lip and spoke in an impression of Jennie. "*They're a part of my look, okay?*"

Jennie downed her drink and spun to look sharply at him. "Well, at least I don't look like Marge-fucking-Simpson with a stupid hat on my head. What is that, anyway? Why do meat-eaters need to wear chimney brushes on their heads?"

Worthington blustered. "It's 'Beefeater,' you wretch. We've been over this. I can't control the clothes I *died* in. This is me and what I wear now. I've come to terms with dying in uniform, and so should you."

Jennie was about to reply when she saw the curious stare from the man Worthington had climbed into. "Everything okay, ma'am?"

The man had a kind face, with the right amount of stubble to make him appear rugged. He wore a dark-blue shirt with the first two buttons open and had gray eyes, which now studied her intently.

Jennie blushed. More than the man's good looks, she found herself melting at his accent. After spending most of her life in the UK and its surrounding partners in Europe, it was refreshing to hear an American accent firsthand.

Jennie nodded. "Yes, everything's fine. I just have some inner demons who need exorcising."

"Rude." Worthington sighed. "And I'd appreciate if you didn't look *through* me at your man-toy."

"Don't we all." The man laughed, then leaned forward and shook her hand. "Jamie."

"Jennie."

Jamie offered to buy Jennie a drink, and before long, that had turned into several. He was nice, telling her about his day job as a merchant banker in the big city and the stresses the job brought. They spoke about his bitch of an ex—his words, not hers—and how he just wanted to settle down with a nice woman and live the family life.

When he asked Jennie about her job, she reeled off the line she had repeated so many times over the years that she didn't even need to think before she said it.

"I'm a researcher of sorts. I travel around the world and track down artifacts that were lost and need to be found and identified."

Jamie grinned. "So, there goes the whole settling-down deal."

Jennie returned the smile. "Oh, sweetie. If you're looking for someone to settle down with, maybe don't look at a random woman in a bar and offer to buy her a drink. You're better than that."

Jamie nodded. He raised two fingers at the bartender, and a moment later, two more shots were in front of them.

"So, go on then, Ms. Researcher. What treasures are there in New York that brought you all the way across the Pond to the land of the free?"

He stared into her eyes, clearly taken by her charms. Then again, most men were. Behind him, an impatient Worthington waved his hands furiously, his expression screaming, "Don't say a word!"

"I'm here to seek out an ancient cult." Jennie smirked. "There have been rumors and sightings of some, well, questionable practices that date back to the late 1600s."

Jamie leaned back and moved a hand to his head. He wobbled as he tried to sit up straight. "Wow, sounds exciting. Isn't that around the time of the Salem witch trials?"

A sparkle appeared in Jennie's eyes. "Oh, a history major?"

Jamie shrugged. "Minor, actually. I majored in accounting and took history to keep me sane."

Worthington scoffed. "He took *history* to keep sane?"

"I *love* history," Jennie replied facetiously. She leaned forward, chin resting on her hand. "You can't imagine how far back my lineage goes."

Jamie leaned closer, his eyes moving to her lips. "Oh, really? How far?"

And then they were kissing. His breath tasted of sambuca and something else she couldn't identify. They locked lips, hands searching each other furiously, and before they knew it, they were out the door and hailing a cab to his apartment.

The night was a hazy blur of passion. Jennie moaned and rolled and writhed until there was nothing left to give. When

Jamie tapped out and fell asleep, she got dressed in a heartbeat and headed out the door.

The streets were dimly lit as she strolled through the city, her head feeling light and clear after her workout at Jamie's apartment. She took a deep breath, familiarizing herself with the sounds and smells of New York.

The thing she loved the most was the precision of the city. Streets laid out in blocks, each an almost perfect square, which made the whole place easier to navigate. Judging from the nearby street sign, she was only a few blocks away from her place. If she was lucky, she'd be back before sunup.

"I see you're not going to bother waiting for me?"

Jennie rolled her eyes, a smug expression on her face. "Oh, Worthington. I didn't see you there."

"That joke gets old pretty quick."

She grinned. "So do you."

"Correction: specters don't age, and you know that." He caught up with her and moved ahead, walking backward to face her. His body floated through any obstacles he passed: hydrants, streetlights, people. "Are you going to tell me what the hell all that was back there?"

She shrugged. "A bit of fun?"

"Oh, 'a bit of fun,' she says. You do recall that the queen sent you over here to deal with a *crisis*? And there you are, gallivanting around with the first US hunk who decides to say hello to you in a bar."

Jennie let out an exasperated sigh. Across the street, she spied another specter, this one a large woman in a nightgown, with her hair in curlers. She floated lazily by, casting a curious look at Jennie and Worthington as they passed each other.

Jennie stared at her longingly, wondering what it would be like to have a *choice* about her specters. To not be bound by whatever pick the queen threw at her. Even to have a specter who gave her a spare few minutes to play without being shadowed and watched.

Worthington continued, "You know I'm going to have to report this behavior? I don't want to, but it's my job to ensure that you're concentrating on your task at hand. To keep you accountable."

"That's *not* your job," Jennie snapped. "Your job is to support and provide me with the powers I need to get the job done. You're nothing more than a corporeal bag of tricks designed to make my job easier so I can do the shit that I need to get done. The minute you start forgetting that, this whole thing falls apart."

Worthington's mouth fell open. He paused in the street. "If *that's* what you think this relationship is, then you're in for a *big* surprise, Genevieve."

Jennie glared at him. "Don't you *dare* call me that."

Worthington took a step back, hands defensively held in the air. "Okay, okay. My fault. We've spoken about this."

Jennie rolled her eyes and took a left down the avenue.

When they came to a small alley that opened up on the right, Jennie slowed down. She could hear grunts and the telltale sounds of fists on flesh. She poked her head around the corner and saw two scrawny thugs laying into a homeless man laid out between bags of trash.

"Another day, another arse-kicking," Jennie muttered, shaking her head to clear some of the effects of the alcohol.

She stepped into the opening of the alley and cupped her hands to her mouth. "Oi, dickweeds. You've got about ten seconds to go before I come over there and show you what it's like to get your arses handed to you."

The thugs stood up straight, their dark eyes leering at Jennie from underneath their hoods.

"Oh, look. The pretty lady wants to fight." The first thug laughed. "Hey, darling? Why don't you leave the fun stuff to the men, eh? Go on your way before we decide to use you as a human piñata."

"We're going to hit her with a stick?" the second thug asked.

The first thug pinched his eyebrows. "No, you idiot. We're going to use *our* sticks on her." He glanced down at his crotch.

"A reference to the Latin culture," Worthington informed Jennie. "A children's game involving hitting a papier-mâché animal—sometimes a donkey or a horse—that has been filled with sweets and strung from a tree, with a stick. What a diverse choice of threat."

"Was that necessary?" Jennie asked.

"Who's she talking to?" thug number two asked in confusion.

The first thug punched his partner in the arm. "How the fuck should I know?"

The homeless man groaned and clutched his side. He coughed and spat up a thick glob of something Jennie didn't want to see.

She glanced at an imaginary watch. "I'm sorry, gentlemen, but time's up. Consider yourself lucky. I don't often give people extra seconds to appreciate their legs."

"Appreciate their… What's she talking about?"

The second thug shut up as Jennie sprinted down the alley and came straight for him. She jumped at the wall, pushed off with one leg, and landed a kick in the man's chest with the other.

The second thug flew backward, stopping when his back smacked into a nearby dumpster with enough force to bend the metal rim.

"A dirty move from a dirty girl." The first thug sneered. "Too bad you've lost the element of surprise."

He ran at Jennie with his fists raised. He aimed a punch at her cheek, but she blocked it easily with her forearm. She waited for his next punch, then, when his guard was lowered, she raised her knee and sank it into his groin.

The thug doubled over and clutched his aching testicles.

Jennie took a step back as the second thug came back at her, his face twisted into lunacy.

"You bitch—"

Another kick to the stomach cut off his rant. He fell flat on his back, winded.

"Let me know when you boys have had enough," Jennie told them. "I've been doing this for far longer than either of you could possibly imagine."

The first thug clutched his crotch and looked at Jennie darkly, then drew the blade at his side and slashed at her midsection. Jennie took a step back, the blade missing her by an inch. He swiped again and Jennie took another step back, feeling the wall behind her.

"Nowhere left to go," the thug growled, a glint of gold appearing as a chain unfurled from around his neck. "First, we'll cripple you, then we'll fuck you. How's that sound?"

Worthington appeared behind the thug, looking ridiculous in his bright red jacket with gold buttons, his fluffy black hat sprouting from his head.

Jennie stifled a laugh. "It's funny that you think you can take little old me down. You know, I'm old enough to be your grandma."

The thug paused, confused.

"Actually, more than likely his great-great-grandma," Worthington put in.

"Way to make a woman feel old," Jennie replied.

The thug looked over his shoulder. "Who are you talking to?"

"Oh, no one," Jennie told them. "Come on. You were going to stab me, weren't you?"

The man's face steeled. He drove the knife forward and gasped as the metal of the blade hit the brick wall behind her with such force that a spike of pain shot into his hand. He shook his wrist, feeling the early onset of the sprain as Jennie laughed at him.

He looked down with sudden amazement, not quite believing what he was seeing.

Jennie's entire midsection had disappeared, having faded as though she were made of nothing more than mist. The upper half of her body was there, and so were her legs, but everything in between was gone.

"Wha…wha… *Impossible,*" he exclaimed.

The second thug was climbing back to his feet when he saw what his companion was looking at. "Ghost!" He spun on his heel and sprinted down the alley, disappearing around the corner in seconds.

Jennie laughed, staring at the first thug with a hardened look on her face. "What's it going to be? Did you want to have another try, or are you going to admit defeat?"

Before the man could make a decision, glass exploded in a shower of fragments around the crown of his head. His eyes crossed and he collapsed to the floor, revealing the homeless man standing behind him with the neck of a bottle in his hand.

The homeless man's face was bruised, and blood dribbled from his lips. He glanced down at Jennie's midsection, wondering what the fuss was about. He could see nothing out of the ordinary—just flat abs like iron underneath her brown leather corset.

Jennie grinned. "See something you like?"

He coughed. "Thank you for your help. You didn't have to do that."

"I did." Jennie placed a hand on his shoulder. "You deserve better than to be ambushed and attacked by two pieces of shit like that. Here." She reached into her pocket and pulled out some cash. "Maybe this will make this night a little more memorable in a good way." She thumbed through her notes and handed over $300 in $50 bills. "Book a hotel for the night and live in luxury for a little. Or invest in something you love. Whatever you do, it's yours."

The man's eyes lit up. "You don't have to, really."

Jennie waved his words away. "It's nothing. I can spare a few quid to make someone's night better."

The man's eyebrow arched. "Quid?"

"Yeah, you know, 'Spare a few bob?' 'Here's a couple of quid?'"

The man looked at her blankly.

Jennie laughed. "It just means money." She placed the bills in his hand and closed his fingers around them. "Consider it a gift from a stranger who just wants to see you happy."

The man's eyes filled with tears. With many thank yous, he grabbed his small plastic sack of belongings and left the alley in search of somewhere to stay the night that didn't stink of piss and moldy leftovers.

Jennie smiled as she stood at the alley's entrance and watched the homeless man almost skip down the street.

"You know that cash was meant for your mission," Worthington told Jennie flatly as he appeared beside her once more.

Jennie rolled her eyes, wishing she could punch the specter in the face. "Oh, I'm sorry. Is doing good deeds against the queen's creed now? I didn't realize I couldn't offer some dough to a man in need. Besides, it's my money, okay? You think over a hundred years of investments haven't made me any profits?"

Worthington wrinkled his nose. "I'm just saying, be careful what you spend your money on. We don't all have unlimited cash."

"Oh, behave, grandpa."

"You're older than me!" Worthington shouted.

Jennie grinned. "Maybe I should be giving *you* advice."

"I highly doubt it. Not until you start acting your age."

"I am acting with the maturity of a woman of my temperament and looks."

Worthington snorted indelicately. "Your temper is always set to *high*."

"That's my point." Jennie threw her hands in the air. "Even with a see-through head, you can still put two brain cells together at times. Why you continue to push me on this maturity thing is beyond me."

"Because I lack a body, not a will," he replied.

Jennie began walking down the street. She shut up as they passed a young woman out on her own, clutching her jacket tight around her, legs sticking out of her miniskirt like pins.

When they were alone again, she continued, "I should just exorcise you right out of my life."

Worthington laughed. "With what, jazzercise? If you could exorcise me, I would be resting against a tree, eating an apple in the afterlife instead of dealing with you and your compulsive tendencies."

"Keep it up, and you might push me far enough to do it."

"As if, Rouge."

Jennie looked around as if expecting someone to be watching her from afar. She saw that the street was empty. "It's *Rogue*," she told him softly,

"Well, my mistake." Worthington smirked, clearly pleased to have put some color in Jennie's cheeks. "Apparently, this afterlife is claiming my sensibilities and memories."

They rounded a corner, and the famous Plaza Hotel came into view. Lights decorated the outside of the hotel like a Christmas tree, and the doorman waited patiently out front.

Jennie wove her way in and entered the elevator, glad to find it empty. She shook her head. "What did I do to deserve you again?"

Worthington chuckled. "Easy. Your last specter got herself excommunicated by the Church, and consequently exorcised."

Jennie frowned. "Oh, yeah, damn. She and I had some great times."

"I suggest that next time, you don't write those good times down in a tell-all book about the Church fathers in Romania."

"How was I supposed to know they could read English?" she argued.

"Also, R.O. Gue was not the smartest pen name."

"I was drunk when we did that…"

"If you truly drank as often as you claim in your stories, you would have consumed more vodka than the amount of air you breathe."

"That's a lot of vodka."

"Truly."

Jennie crossed the thirteenth-floor foyer and unlocked her apartment door, revealing the glitz and glamour the Plaza offered. She walked into the living area and immediately kicked off her shoes as she headed over to the minibar. She unscrewed the lid of a mini bottle of vodka and drained the contents.

Worthington sat in an armchair and kicked his booted feet onto an ottoman. "That only goes to prove my point."

Jennie glared at him.

Worthington ignored the look. "And once you're finished getting well and truly trollied, what do you propose then? This whole evening has been a waste from start to finish."

"Not entirely," Jennie slurred, wiping her mouth with the back of her arm.

Worthington cocked an eyebrow and waited expectantly.

"In case you didn't notice, those two thugs were wearing chains around their neck."

"Oh, wonderful. I wonder who they stole those from."

"They both had the symbol of Mjölnir on them," Jennie continued as if Worthington hadn't uttered a word. "Thor's hammer? The sign of the Spectral Plane? You know what that means, right?"

Worthington's smile fell away.

"It means we're in the right neighborhood. If the grunts of the Spectral Plane are nearby, their bosses will be, too."

Worthington shook his head, letting out a small laugh. "You son-of-a—"

"Stop," Jennie interrupted, beaming. "You know it's not proper to abuse a lady."

She opened another vodka and drained it in one.

CHAPTER TWO

Jennie's hangover shifted a little after midday.

"You'd think after over a century, you'd have found a cure by now," Worthington complained, giving her a derisive look.

"Don't get me started," Jennie retorted. She sidestepped around an old woman using a walker and adjusted her sunglasses, just one measure she adopted to help her cope with bright lights and woozy mornings. The streets were packed with people as the sun beat down on the pair of them.

Worthington floated through the people, leaving all of them with the slightest of chills down their spines.

"You know, I thought we were really making a breakthrough when Coke was invented. Liquid sugar in a drink. That had to be it, right?"

Worthington frowned. "When Coke was… I thought you said you were born in '81? Wouldn't that have made you a little girl? Coke came around in the late 1800s, after all."

Jennie waited for the green light to appear, then crossed the street with the others. She looked at Worthington, impressed. "Wow, someone's been studying their history."

A balding man with multiple chins standing directly behind

Worthington gave Jennie a strange look. She stifled a laugh and abruptly sped up.

"Well, you get a lot of time to read when you're living as a specter in the eternal afterlife. Read and think. Read and think. Then read and think some more." He sighed. "So, your first hangover was when you were, what? Five? Six?"

Jennie took a left. This street was lined with expensive-looking shops, cafes, and restaurants, all flooded with people in the throes of the lunchtime rush.

"No, nothing like that. I was actually thirteen. Turns out, it's pretty easy to steal liquor when your friends in the afterlife lend you a helping hand." She spotted what she was looking for up ahead. "Aha! Speaking of which."

She jogged through the crowd and fell in line a few feet back from a muscular black man with dark suspenders holding his trousers up and a short-sleeved brown shirt. He was taller than the rest of the crowd, with a bowler hat sitting slightly askew on the top of his head.

But that wasn't what had drawn Jennie's attention. It wasn't even the revolver in the holster on his hip, or the large, ancient socket wrench he held over his shoulder like the handle of a bindle.

The man glowed with the faint ethereal indication of a specter.

They trailed him down Sixth Avenue for a few blocks, always remaining far enough away to not draw attention to themselves.

He took another left onto Fifty-First, where the streets were quieter. Now it was them, the man, and just a smattering of people on the streets. When he approached an alley on his right, he took the turn and ducked inside.

"It's always alleys, isn't it?" Worthington muttered.

Jennie sped up, afraid to lose him, but when she turned around the corner, the specter was nowhere to be seen.

Jennie threw her hands in the air. "Damn specters."

"Actually, the damned aren't specters. They're poltergeists."

"You think I don't know that?" Jennie retorted.

A passing woman glanced down the alley, curious as to who Jennie was shouting at.

Jennie fell silent and took a breath. She strolled deeper into the alley and narrowed her eyes, allowing her body to try to sense the direction of the specter.

Worthington stood beside her, wincing as she drew power from him.

It came to her, like true north on a compass. She stared at the wall of the large building before her and placed a hand on the brickwork. "Worthington, if you wouldn't mind?"

"When have you ever asked my permission before?"

Worthington dutifully marched beside Jennie as her power reached out and connected with the specter. She felt a slight chill at the connection. She closed her eyes, took a step forward, and felt herself become immaterial. The sensation was not unpleasant. When she opened her eyes again, she was in a small, dark room.

People chattered somewhere nearby. A piano was playing. A group of women warmed up their vocal cords with a variety of exercises designed to test their range.

Jennie exited the room, allowing light to spill into the small storage cupboard. She followed the long corridor beyond, keeping her body attuned to the trail of the specter. She passed doors with names decorated in strings of lights but saw none she recognized. It was from these that the voices rang.

As she neared the end of the corridor, a door opened on her left and a woman stepped out backward, still speaking to whoever was in the room. "She'll understand when she realizes what it takes to be a star. You can't work with amateurs until—"

She bumped into Jennie.

"Oh, sorry." She eyed Jennie as she spoke between chews of

her gum. "*Nice.*" She nodded approvingly. "Did they up the budget for costumes this year?"

Jennie stifled a laugh. "Something like that."

The woman poked her head back inside the room. "See, Diane? *This* is what a professional looks like." Back to Jennie. "Break a leg out there, honey."

The woman marched down the hallway and knocked loudly on a door farther down.

"She's a strange sort," Worthington remarked.

Jennie saw the small logo on the corner of the names on the doors and felt herself swell with excitement. "Worthington, do you realize where we are?"

"Somewhere actors come to die?"

Jennie shot him a look. "We're at Radio City Music Hall. I've *always* wanted to visit here."

"Well, you've picked a lovely time," Worthington replied dryly. "Maybe you should get some tickets for a show, put your feet up, take your time, and just dilly-dally until Christmas rolls around. I'm sure the queen would be more than happy to finance your excursion."

But Jennie wasn't listening. As she opened the door from the theater dressing rooms, the sounds of classical music filled the air. Wooden boards beneath her feet indicated she was at the back of the stage, and several props cloaked in the shadows confirmed it.

There was a crease in the enormous maroon curtain. Jennie peered through it and saw a handsome man in a tuxedo playing the piano. His eyes were shut as he fell into the music, and he played as though his heart was full.

Sitting in the row of seats in front of the stage was a man with his hands steepled in front of his face. Two women sat beside him, furiously scribbling notes on the clipboards in their laps.

Jennie was instantly thrown back to her own days as a child, growing up in London around the boom of the modern theater scene. Her parents had worked at the Savoy Theater. It was one of London's largest and finest underground theaters, the one which had led the way on the installation of electric lights to improve safety in the productions.

That was a blessing that had been long overdue, given the number of accidents caused by enthusiastic flames in candles as they ate up and destroyed their wooden homes in seconds.

Back then, Jennie had been nothing more than a little girl, wandering around the stage while impatient directors tapped their feet and adoring actors swooned and laughed. The Savoy had become a second home to her, a place that filled her with warmth, delight, and song.

It had also been the place she'd first discovered her gift. A theater as old as the Savoy had been the target of rumors of ghosts and ghouls for as long as people could remember. And, while others thought they were mere superstition, it turned out that they made pretty decent playmates.

Even after all these years, Jennie wondered what might have happened if instead of ghosts, she'd had the chance to play with scripts and test her talents on stage. Of course, being the paranormal queen's number-one killing machine was fun, but would she ever get the chance to play Juliet? Lady Macbeth? To read from Beckett, Chekov, or Andrew Lloyd Webber?

"It sure is beautiful, isn't it?"

Jennie spun around and saw the man they had been following studying a speaker the height of a double fridge.

The man stared admiringly at it, craning behind to get to the control panel. "An HR-2190. Man, these things make the HR-2170 look like a TCX-16. Imagine if we'd had these back in my day. We could've boomed some folks' skeletons right out of their skin."

Worthington arched an eyebrow. "I'm sorry, are you talking in some kind of code? I have literally no idea what you're talking about."

The man laughed, his face kind and warm. "Don't worry about it, chimney sweep." He pulled an ethereal cloth from his pocket and wiped his hands, a habit carried over from his time. "Name's Baxter. Baxter Scampton. We don't often see people of your..." He paused as he studied Worthington's attire. "Um, origin, on this side of the Pond."

"Yes, well, there are a lot of things going on at the minute which haven't been seen on 'this side of the Pond,'" Jennie replied, folding her arms. "Which is why we've come."

Baxter took a step back in surprise. "She can talk?"

Worthington nodded. "The trick is getting her to shut up."

"You better watch your tone," she told the specter, pointing a finger at him. "Of course, I can talk. I've been able to talk since I was two years old. I think what you *meant* to say is, 'She can talk to specters?'"

Baxter chuckled, a disbelieving look in his eyes. "Well, I'll be damned. You guys are springing up everywhere at the moment, aren't you?"

"What are you talking about?" Jennie asked. "'You guys?'"

"Hey! Who's back there?" The director shouted from the front row. "We can hear you! Lucy, run behind the curtains and tell whoever's back there that they're out of showbiz for good! No one interrupts Don Apatow's rehearsals and gets away with it!"

"I think that's our cue to leave," Baxter told them hurriedly.

Jennie nodded. "Lead the way."

Worthington followed. "Spiffing."

Baxter led them through a door at the side of the stage and up several flights of stairs. They eventually came out at a small empty bar which later that night would be packed with avid theater enthusiasts ready to watch the latest Don Apatow spectacular.

Jennie locked the door. Worthington and Baxter took their seats, laughing as they exhaled and slumped into the plush comfort.

Jennie crossed the room and ducked behind the bar, emerging a moment later with a handful of bottles.

"I don't think you're meant to touch those," Baxter warned her.

Worthington waved a hand. "She doesn't care."

"Hey, you know what'd be good?" Jennie examined the labels of the bottles. "A stiff Lapinsky."

"What's that?" Baxter asked, watching Jennie with interest.

Jennie worked her way around the bar, grabbing spirit measures and weighing fruits in her hand. "Something that went out of style a few decades ago. Vodka, lime, orange juice, rum, and a dash of Boku. It was named after Richard Lewis' wife—y'know, the comedian with the squiffy hair? I told him it'd never catch on, and guess who was right?"

Worthington sat forward. "When did you meet Richard Lewis?"

"Remember the tour he did in the late nineties?"

"We're talking the twentieth century now, right?" Baxter asked.

"That's the one," Jennie confirmed. "I went to watch the show and bumped into him backstage afterward. Nice guy. Think he was only after a quickie, but he underestimated how well I can hold my liquor."

She rifled through the fridges, searching for something to finish off her concoction. "Ah, here we go." She found a small peeler and scored a section of skin from a lime. The peel curled like a ribbon, and she poured her cocktail into a tall glass. Condensation beaded the outside and small bubbles filtered to the top.

She took a long sip. "My goodness, I forgot how great they were. Would either of you like one?" She laughed, knowing that specters had a different digestive system than mortals.

She drained half the glass through a straw, poured the rest from the shaker into the glass to top up, then sat down with the others. "Splendid. Now that we're suitably refreshed, are you going to tell us what a specter such as yourself is doing getting all pervy on a speaker system at Radio City Music Hall?"

"I wasn't perving," Baxter denied. "Truth is that I'm an inventor. Well, I *was* an inventor back in 1908 until a little accident parted my soul from my body, and now—voila!—here I am. I like to check out modern gadgetry to see what kind of technological advances are happening with the world."

Worthington's lip curled. "So, you thought you'd start by staring at a speaker?"

"It's not *just* a speaker," Baxter replied, getting a little heated. "The Music Hall just updated their sound system. An entirely new spec of the latest audio engineering designed to give full, three-sixty-degree sound that distributes evenly around its theater. Do you know how difficult that is?"

Worthington shrugged.

"I'm guessing it's difficult?" Jennie answered.

Baxter nodded enthusiastically. "*So* difficult! If we'd have had this technology when I was alive and well, maybe so many of my relatives wouldn't have suffered from hearing problems throughout the years." He shook his head, his eyes going glassy. "Maximum bass, and a rich sound with none of the damage."

"Wonderful," Jennie remarked without much enthusiasm.

Baxter's attention turned back to Jennie, his eyes trailing from her face to her hips.

"Hey, pervert, my eyes are up here."

Worthington rolled his eyes. "She says, wearing a corset."

"It's not a corset," Jennie corrected. "It's a 'focus strap.'"

"Oh, here we go."

Baxter chuckled. "What's a focus strap?"

"Pain helps me focus." Jennie smirked, peeking over the top of her sunglasses. "And this is one way to keep me in a permanent state of pain." She chewed her lip. "Plus, it makes my tits look great."

"Why do you need to be in a permanent state of pain?" Baxter asked, narrowly dodging the hook.

"Oh, no." Jennie wagged a finger. "You need to answer my questions first. You said 'guys like me' were springing up everywhere. What did that mean?"

Baxter scratched his chin. "People who can communicate with specters. People who can dabble with us 'lifers.'"

"Lifers?" Worthington asked.

"A nickname we call each other on this side of the Pond," he explained.

"It's not a Pond," Jennie interjected. "It's an ocean. Unless you think you could fit that body of water in someone's garden?"

"Anyway." Baxter grinned. "In all my years of living in this form, I've met only one or two folks who were even half-close to being able to see and communicate with the dead, but in the last few months, there have been reports of people who can sense and summon the dead. I mean, none to the extent that you can, as far as I'm aware. But still. Something's been happening. Something's changed."

He stared intensely at Jennie, holding her gaze with a small smile on his face. "I still can't believe you can see me."

"Yes, it's a real miracle," Jennie agreed, sounding bored. She turned to Worthington. "Do you think these people might have something to do with the rising number of specters in the city?"

Worthington shrugged. "I'd say it's definitely a good place to start."

Baxter sat up. "Hold on. Now that you've heard my part, maybe you can answer my questions. You know, it's not often I get a chance to speak to a mortal. At least, not one who can reply to me."

"You're better off keeping her quiet," Worthington told him dryly. "And 'mortal' might be too strong a word for Jennie."

"Either way, what's a couple of British folks doing on our side of the Po—" He wilted under Jennie's glare. "Ocean, following a specter into the back of a nationally recognized theater?"

Jennie's eyebrow raised. "You knew we were following you?"

"I had my suspicions, especially when old fur-head there was bobbing along with his hat poking out like a goddamn beacon."

"*Hey*," Worthington snapped. "This is the official uniform of the royal guard of the monarchs of England. At least, it was at the time I passed on. They've updated the current uniform somewhat; removed some of the fancier details, which I highly disagree with. But still! Do not mock what should be respected—*must* be respected—by the specters who fall under the rule of Her Majesty and the paranormal court."

"The paranormal court?" Baxter's eyes widened. "You two are from the paranormal court?"

Jennie crossed one leg over the other, twirling her Lapinsky in one hand. "Not only that, but we've been sent here on a very important mission, and it sounds like you might be the perfect specter to help us."

CHAPTER THREE

<u>Brooklyn, New York, Present Day</u>

"What you're about to see is a secret to anyone outside of the spectral circle," Baxter told Jennie and Worthington as he took the pair down a narrow side street.

Night had fallen, which was Jennie's preferred time of operation. When the streets were dark and the honest and true were tucked up tightly in their beds, it was much easier to sniff out the filth.

Bad guys operated in darkness, for the most part. That was the truth of it. It was no wonder that children's stories of monsters and demons often portrayed the fabled creatures in the dark beneath their bed and inside their closets.

Carpe Noctem, Jennie thought, choosing not to let herself get distracted by the drug deal she could see clearly in a nearby alley. If they were stupid enough to ingest poisons into their system, they were dumb enough to risk the chances of dying from them.

They arrived at a small wooden door. "Here we are."

"What is this place?" Jennie asked, staring up at redbrick walls covered in graffiti.

"A place for communion." Baxter grinned, disappearing through the door. "Come on."

Jennie connected with Worthington and took a step through the door, feeling herself become immaterial. She passed through the wood and followed Baxter down a set of stone steps leading deep into the underground.

More and more murmuring voices greeted them, the farther down they went. The bare stone walls were chilly, and a slight funk hung in the air, offending Jennie's nostrils.

"What's that smell?" she asked.

Baxter laughed. "Cheese. This place is used as a cheese-maturing facility in the daytime. Fortunately for us specters, that's something that we don't have to worry much about. Our sense of smell is—"

"Less accurate than a human's," Jennie finished.

Baxter nodded and smiled.

When they reached the bottom of the stairs, they went through a doorway and into a room that looked like it might once have been a part of the city's catacomb system. Wooden shelves labeled with various names of cheeses lined the walls. Some were in bags, some out in the open in wheels, and some hung from strings.

Weaving lazily between the catacombs was one of the largest gatherings of specters Jennie had ever seen.

They came from all time periods. There were some dressed in the plain, shabby garb of peasants from the 1700s. Many wore the uniform of the soldiers of the American Revolution, complete with muskets. Some had the powdered faces and wigs of the aristocracy.

Then there were the men, women, and children from the twentieth and twenty-first centuries. Some wore flat black caps, and others wore flares and open-collared shirts. There were even a few gangsters milling around with cigars in their mouths and guns holstered at their sides.

"Quite the collection," Jennie remarked. "Who are all these people?"

"I call them the 'neutrals,'" Baxter replied quietly. "The specters from the city who just want to socialize and tell their tales. The ghosts who are happy living in the middle and want a safe space to drink, be merry, and shoot the shit."

"Bax!" A woman in a power suit with blonde hair cropped at her shoulders approached Baxter and greeted him with a kiss to each cheek. She was slender, with the gaunt look of someone who had failed to get the right nutrition into her body when she'd been alive.

"Eva," Baxter replied. Eva's enthusiasm was clearly one-sided. "I'd like you to meet some new friends of mine. This is Worthington."

"Pleased to meet you," Worthington offered, taken aback as Eva leaned forward and kissed both cheeks.

Jennie introduced herself before Worthington could drop her full name. "Please, call me Jennie."

Eva moved to kiss her cheeks but paused to study Jennie. She leaned conspiratorially toward Baxter. "Is she…"

"A human, yeah."

"But she…"

"Spoke to you, yeah. She can see us all." He turned to Jennie to check. "Can't you?"

Jennie nodded, a smug grin on her face. "Crystal clear."

"There! See?"

"How come I haven't met these two before?" Eve sounded hurt, as though Jennie and Worthington were competition for her affections. "Where did you meet them?"

"We're new to the city," Jennie explained. "We've come by orders of the que—"

"Er, the questing crew of yore." Baxter laughed, cutting Jennie off. "That's right, they're here to do some research in the city and take back what they learn about the spectral community to their homeland. Isn't that right?"

"Riiight," Jennie replied.

"Well, you couldn't have come at a better time," Eva told her, puffing on her eternal cigarette. "With shit going down how it is in the city, you'll be able to fill reams of paper with notes." She leaned closer. "I'm telling you, it's a full-blown turf war. I saw it myself back in my mortal days. It's East Side versus West Side all over again. Listen to hip-hop from the nineties. You'll get what I mean."

"Turf wars?" Worthington asked.

"That's actually why we've come," Baxter told Eve. "Have you seen Tobias around anywhere? We've got some questions to ask him."

"Tobias?" Eve repeated blankly.

Baxter sighed. "You know, the big guy with the gold chain around his neck. Tattoos on his face?"

Eva shook her head.

"Massive bullet wounds to the chest and arms," he continued in a beleaguered tone.

"Oh!" She slapped her forehead. "I think I saw him over with the Teller Twins, trying to work out the best way to haunt his ex-wife. Just two weeks after his death, and she's already shacking up with his best friend. Talk about moving on fast."

Baxter thanked Eva and said his goodbyes before leading Jennie and Worthington through the crowd.

It was strange watching the specters. Somehow it was like being at a cocktail party, except the people could only bring what they had with them when they'd died. Jennie had seen specters able to solidify enough to pick up objects and move them around, but none who could drink the concoctions of mortals.

What sad lives they must lead. I'd be devastated if I couldn't at least shake a shaker and make something fresh and new for my tongue to enjoy.

New. That was getting harder and harder to find the more years that she lived. There were only so many tastes in the world.

Jennie did her best to avoid the gazes of the specters around her as they crossed the room. She knew she stuck out like a sore thumb, but that didn't mean she had to draw attention to herself.

Not that walking behind a Beefeater with a bearskin hat which scraped the fucking ceiling draws any attention away from me. Why did the queen have to give me him *of all people?*

They found Tobias standing in a corner of a room in a heated discussion with two men who were identical to look at. Tobias wore an expensive-looking suit with a white rose on the lapel, his midsection sunken in toward the place where his chest had caved from the bullets that killed him. His arm had several chunks missing, as though someone had taken bites from him.

The twin men wore red and green cardigans, respectively, and beige corduroys. Their hair was combed neatly to the side, the pair easily looking as though they could have been the stars of a TV commercial from the 1950s.

"I'm telling you, I tried that. The bitch just doesn't believe in ghosts."

The twins stared at him. "Not even when objects are floating above her head in the middle of the night?"

"No, she just thinks it's a goddamn dream."

"Well," the twin in the red cardigan complained, "there go my plans for teaching Spectral Haunting 101."

"I thought you guys scared your wives so badly, they ended up killing themselves. How did you do it?"

"Oh, that was easy." The one in green chuckled. "We just appeared in the mirror every time they looked. Couple that with passing through them every few minutes to freak out their adrenaline system, and you're golden."

The twin in red nodded. "Plus, it helped when we found out they were both going on a weekend away to help heal themselves from their mourning and we cut the brake lines to their car."

"Oh, yeah," Green Cardigan replied, staring into the distance as if remembering it all with fondness. "They wrapped around that tree so many times, the ambulance had to peel them off with tongs."

"Why would you murder your wives after you died?" Jennie asked before she could stop herself.

The twins gave her a strange look. "Because *they* murdered *us*," they replied at the same time. They lifted their tops to reveal wounds on their chests where the knives had plunged into them. "The bitches had it coming."

A woman floated past them, her face and body warped and out of shape. "You could've chosen a nicer way to do it," she put in before disappearing back into the crowd.

Red Cardigan looked at Green Cardigan. "See what I mean? Bee-yotch."

"Have you tried swapping their sugar for salt?" Baxter offered.

Tobias pinched the bridge of his nose. "You realize I'm not after schoolyard pranks or murder here. I want to piss the bitch off." He shook his head and sighed. "Just forget it. What do you want, Bax?"

"Nice way to greet an old friend." Baxter smirked. "I'd like to introduce you to two friends of mine, Worthington and Jennie."

Tobias looked at the pair for the first time. "You want to be careful, lad, walking around here dressed like that. Some might take offense to your costume. Get the wrong idea."

Worthington huffed. "It's *not* a costume."

"Yeah, yeah." Tobias waved a hand. "Just know that there are many here that aren't exactly proponents of the queen's rule. This is a safe space for the neutrals to talk and be free." He turned to Baxter. "And bringing mortals into this place? Is that a smart move?"

"Probably a better idea than talking about me like I'm not here," Jennie replied. "Man, you specters are up your own arses, aren't you? Thinking you're the only ones around here who can hear you."

Tobias' mouth fell open. "You've found one?"

Baxter considered this. "More like she found me. That's why we're here. You told me the other day that you've seen other humans who can communicate with specters. Can you tell us where?"

Tobias sat back in his chair, processing this information. He studied Jennie's body.

"Hey, numbnuts. My eyes are up here," Jennie told him sharply, causing his spectral cheeks to color.

Jennie rolled her eyes. "Even in the afterlife, all men are the same."

Tobias chuckled. "I like her."

Baxter grinned. "Me too."

Worthington scoffed. "The charm fades after a while, I assure you."

Tobias fixed Jennie with dark eyes. "I don't know how much help I can be, other than to say that, yeah, I saw another person like you. A small fellow with a fucked-up face and a hood to try to hide it. I thought he was one of us at first until I saw the other humans talking to him. Gathered in a circle, they were, in the dark, muttering shit I couldn't quite make out."

"Was there anything…unifying about them?" Jennie asked.

"Unifying?" Tobias repeated.

Jennie nodded. "You know, like anything that could identify them from a distance?"

Tobias thought a moment. "Not that I can think of. It was dark, and if they had anything, it would have been under their black robes."

"So, how do you know this man can communicate with spirits?" Worthington asked, intrigued. "From what I can tell, we've got a bunch of cult followers muttering the words of the Dark Lord and gathering in the darkness. That's nothing unusual."

Tobias met Worthington's eyes. "Because he had his own specter following him like an obedient lapdog." He grinned. "You know what I mean?"

"A *lapdog*?" Worthington exclaimed. "If you don't watch your mouth, I'll make sure—"

"Where did you see these men?" Jennie asked quickly, eager to shut Worthington's mouth.

Tobias spoke to Jennie but stared at Worthington with an amused smirk. "Central Park. They were skirting the edges. Looked like they were trying to find something."

Jennie nodded. "Perfect." She spun on her heel and left without another word.

Worthington followed, leaving Baxter and Tobias flummoxed behind them. Jennie had never been one for frivolities, and as Worthington was eager to point out, they had a job to do.

While Worthington wove through the other specters, Jennie simply walked through them all. Over the years, she had become accustomed to the sensation of passing through their bodies and become numb to the feeling.

As the door was in sight, a gruff voice called to Jennie, "You got somewhere to be, darling? You seem to be in an awful hurry."

Several specters appeared before her, thick with muscle and eyes in which the pupils had dilated so wide that the entire eye was black. A woman who looked like she might once have been a powerlifter blocked her path and folded her arms.

"I am," Jennie replied, ducking her head and expecting to pass through the specters, only to find they had materialized enough to become physical.

"That's a fancy trick," Jennie told them. "You do realize that the more physical you become, the easier it is for me to kick your ass?"

The specters laughed. "You really think that you, a mortal, can hurt us?" the woman asked. "Come off it, darling."

Baxter ran up behind Jennie and Worthington. "What seems to be the problem here?"

"The problem is that this is supposed to be a neutral zone, and *you* have bought in scum from the Winter Court to infect our party. You really think no one would notice Lord Pompous there with his tree of a hat and bright red jacket?" She spat on the floor. "Winter Court bastards. And don't even get me started on the human."

While the woman spoke, Jennie saw Eva's head poking around the corner, an expression of guilt on her face.

"The *Winter Court?*" Worthington snorted. "The *Win—* Madame, you best be careful of how you address the servants of the queen's court. I've heard some nonsense in my day, but this…"

Jennie felt her fuse grow short. The Winter Court was a nickname that those against the rule of the crown had adopted since Victoria had taken over the paranormal court. Unfortunately, that hadn't been because of the court's resemblance to the fabled Faerie Court that had circled Wikipedia and the internet since Jim Butcher's *Dresden Files* first launched in the year 2000, but rather due to the frosty and chilly atmosphere some had claimed had fallen over the spectral world since the queen had taken her throne.

Any mention of such blasphemy angered Jennie, a faithful servant of the court for over a hundred years. "You've got about ten seconds to get out of my way before you force me to do something I'm not likely to regret."

"Oh, really? And what could a mortal possibly do to hurt a specter?" The woman scoffed, much to the delight of the men standing behind her. "You going to exorcise us and send us into the great beyond?"

"You really don't want to test her," Worthington warned as a crowd gathered around them.

"Oooh, I'm shaking in my boots," the woman mocked. She grabbed a handful of Jennie's hair and rose upward.

Jennie felt a blossom of pain from the top of her scalp as she was lifted off the floor. This pain she didn't show, however. Instead, her eyes were closed behind her sunglasses as she silently watched the clock in her head.

Three.

Two.

One.

Oh, bitch. It's on.

CHAPTER FOUR

There was a blinding flash of light, followed by gasps from the crowd.

The woman held her fist in the air, uncertain what was happening as she felt Jennie's weight lessen to nothing. She blinked against the sudden attack of light and turned her head away.

Then came the pain.

The mortal's fist pummeled her cheek before she had any idea what was happening. The next thing she knew, she had toppled backward and was looking at the ceiling from the floor.

She rubbed her sore cheek, not quite believing what had happened. She could feel pain. For the first time in a long time, she actually *hurt*.

The light faded entirely, revealing another specter in the room.

But she isn't another specter, is she? What the fuck is going on?

45

Jennie jumped over the woman on the floor and turned her attention to the guys standing behind her.

She was glowing a spectral blue, a small line of power connecting her to Worthington. From this connection, she channeled the spectral powers she had within and connected with the world of the dead.

"You don't know how many cocky sons-of-bitches I've had to teach lessons to over the years," she told them. "You still sure you want to do this?"

The first specter roared and ran toward her. Jennie blocked his jab with a cross of her forearms, deflecting the shot and using his momentum to sidestep and allow him past. As he drew parallel with her, she raised an elbow and jammed it down on the back of his skull.

The specter cried out in pain and landed on top of the woman, who had been halfway toward getting to her knees.

Jennie wagged a finger at her. "Not yet, pussycat. Stay down until I tell you to get up."

A shout came from the next specter, a man with fists like bowling balls and a face to match. He held a small dagger, which he tossed back and forth between his hands. The grunt next to him did the same, both leering menacingly as they came at her with their knives.

They attacked with impressive ferocity. The first specter slashed at her stomach, and Jennie blocked it while drawing her pistol. Ghostly metal clanged on metal, and the specter responded by attempting to backhand her with his melon of a fist.

Jennie ducked, then used her momentum to drive an uppercut into his chin. When the next specter came at her, she was in the midst of replacing her pistol in its holster. She saw his fist and prepared to duck again, only she reacted a fraction too late.

The fist connected with her shoulder and spun her around.

The blow was hard enough to send her careening into the throng of specters watching like a kids' school fight.

"You okay?" Worthington shouted.

Jennie tilted her head left to right, her bones cracking as she did so. "Yep. No worries."

The specter charged at her, and she allowed his arms to wrap around her waist and drive her back into the brick wall. Had they been on the mortal plane, the bricks would likely have cracked, adding to the rustic antiquity of this place.

Jennie patted the specter's mountainous back. "It's quite fine if you've got mommy issues, you know. Lots of people's mommies never hug their children."

The grunt looked up at her, confusion on his face. "What are you talking about?"

"Nothing," she grinned. "I just wanted to distract you long enough to see what you're about."

"See what I'm— *Argh!*"

The specter's voice cut off as Jennie's eyes grew white behind her glasses. She closed her eyes, feeling around for his power, overriding the string attached to Worthington.

The specter tensed as he felt Jennie's power probing him.

Jennie smiled. "Oh, now this could be interesting…"

She honed her concentration on the specter and felt her body change. The muscles on her arms and legs grew so taut and strong that she felt she could lift anything.

And it seemed she could.

She grabbed the specter around his waist, hugging him tightly as she raised him off the floor; the angle caused him to hang awkwardly in her arms. "Hey, Worthington. Fancy a bite of this beefcake?"

"What are you talking about?" Worthington replied.

Jennie grinned. "You know, because you're a Beefeater?"

Worthington closed his eyes as if pained by her words. He leaned toward the nearest specter—a boy of around thirteen in a flat cap, his cheeks stained with soot—and said, "She thinks that kind of stuff is funny, but all it does is—"

A hand wrapped around his ankle and pulled his leg out from beneath him. Worthington landed on his face.

The woman crawled toward him and licked her lips. "You! You're the traitor who's giving your abilities to that bitch? How about we exorcise you and cut her off from the source? Perhaps that'd make this a fair fight."

Worthington disagreed. "I'm sorry, ma'am, but there's something wrong with a woman who thinks a fair fight is five against one."

The woman spun on the floor and kicked Worthington in the face.

Jennie tossed the specter through the air with ease. She might as well have been launching a paper airplane. The specter whacked into his comrade, and the pair folded to the ground. "How are you doing back there, fuel bag?" She looked across the crowd and saw Worthington on the floor.

Worthington sighed. "Maybe a little help over here."

Jennie ran across the room and stood on the specter's back to launch herself toward the woman, who held a knife and was inching toward Worthington.

She landed on the woman's back, and before she had a chance to respond, reached down to her hip, where a large gun materialized before the specters' eyes. A few of them gasped in awe. It was around the size and shape of a sawed-off shotgun, but the weapon had clearly had some modifications made to it over the years.

"Put. The knife. Down." Jennie punctuated each word with a curl of her lip.

Incredibly, the woman beneath her boot began to wheeze a laugh.

"You really think you can hurt me with *that*? You must be even more stupid than you look. How about when I finally slice your throat, you can crawl back to your precious queen and beg her forgiveness for being such a poor excuse for a mortal? I'm sure she'd like that."

Jennie thumbed off the safety and held the gun inches from the woman's face. "Or how about you beg for forgiveness, and I give you a chance to keep that pretty face in one piece? I think that's a fair enough trade, considering you and your fuck-buddies decided to gang up on us for no reason."

"No reason?" The woman spat again. "The filthy queeny scum says there's no reason? Think again, bitch. You're the whole reason we're in this fucking mess."

Jennie raised an eyebrow. Moved the gun closer. "Say that one more time."

"Go ahead." The woman sneered. "Let's see how well your precious mortal weapons fare against a spec—"

The report was loud, a great booming explosion of sound. The specters covered their ears with their hands, then began complaining of burst eardrums and a high-pitched whine.

Jennie studied the woman's face, a smug smile teasing the corner of her lips.

The specter was still very much "alive," but her head was a complete mess. The only part of her that remained in working order was what was left of her mouth as she protested and cried out in a pain she hadn't believed possible.

Jennie shook her head. It didn't matter how many times she faced off against specters with her modified guns, they never learned. She supposed they grew complacent that their weapons wouldn't work on mortals and assumed that to be the case for anyone who dipped into the spectral world.

It seemed they had no idea that the rules didn't apply to Jennie.

The specters behind her looked at their boss with sudden fear.

"Wha… What are you?" one grunted before they whirled and

headed for the exit, vanishing through the doorway moments later.

A stunned silence fell across the catacombs.

Jennie dropped to one knee beside the woman, looking at the place where her eyes had once been like a lover sitting at the edge of a cancer patient's bed. "Hurts, doesn't it? See, that's what happens to specters who underestimate my capabilities. You might not have found your way to the dark tunnel that comes after the spectral afterlife, but you'll wish you had." She plucked the woman's knife from her hand and examined it. She placed the blade against her forearm and increased the pressure until a tiny droplet of blood formed. "Nice. I'm guessing this is…1940s? Tempered steel? Maybe military-grade?"

The woman nodded.

"Could have really hurt me with that, you know." She tossed the knife onto the woman's body and stood up. "Don't worry, though. Just give it three to five days, and your face will be as good as new. You might not know this, but specters actually have an impressive ability to heal."

The mouth flapped, uttering unintelligible syllables, until finally. "Who…who…"

"Who am I?" Jennie asked, leaning over the woman. "That doesn't really matter right now. All you need to know is that I've been in this game longer than you've been around. I eat specters like you for breakfast and shit them out at dinnertime. But before I go on my almighty rampage, I need to ask you a question. Who are you working for?"

To her surprise, the lower part of the specter's face broke into a smile. She gargled on something in the back of her throat and laughed. "You have no idea who you're up against."

"Why don't you enlighten me?" Jennie pressed.

The woman waved her closer. Jennie leaned toward the woman's mouth. She could hear odd parts of words in a hushed tone, then warm liquid hit her face. A dollop of bloody ghost spit dripped off her cheek.

Jennie stood up, aimed the gun at her head, and took the shot. Had the woman been mortal, there would be nothing left to salvage, but Jennie knew it would all grow back in time.

"Make that seven to ten days," Jennie told her. "Doctor's orders." She nodded for Worthington to follow her and headed for the door, her body still shining with a ghostly pallor.

She rested her hand on the handle and cut off the connection to Worthington. Her body returned to its normal color, the small scratch on her arm now clearer than before. At a wave of his hand, the guns fizzled into nothingness. "Oh, and tell your boss what you've seen. We're coming for him, and whoever his security is, well. It doesn't matter. There's a new law enforcer in this city."

CHAPTER FIVE

New York City, USA, Present Day

Worthington cast furtive glances behind him as Jennie beelined through the streets toward Central Park. "Are you sure that was entirely wise?"

"What do you mean?" Jennie replied.

Worthington gave her a stern look. "You know, informing every specter in New York about what we're here to do and what you're capable of? In my day, we used to run covert missions based on the element of surprise."

Jennie laughed. "Yes, and in your day, you also invaded Vietnam and brought AIDS to the Western world. Things move on. Get with the program. Now those specters are going to be shit-scared and tell their friends about us. My reputation runs on people knowing that I deliver justice—no ifs, ands, or buts. Besides, the sooner we can make an impact, the sooner we can get back to the UK and deliver the good news to the queen."

"Oh, won't that be a blessing," Worthington replied, a far-off dreamy look in his eyes.

Jennie ignored his sarcasm. "Exactly. What do you think all

that stuff they were saying in there was anyway? The Yanks seem awfully hostile toward the paranormal court."

"Not *all* of them," Worthington corrected. "Just a small number. It probably has something to do with the fact that we're not well-represented over here. You know as well as I do that the paranormal court operates out of UK and Europe. It takes a lot of work to provide protection and loyalty to those over on this side of the—"

"Don't say it," Jennie warned.

"The Pond." Worthington smirked.

Jennie glared at him. "Well, let's see if we can catch a few of those traitors and work out what the hell is going on here."

"And if they don't talk?"

Jennie peered over the top of her glasses.

"Riiight." Worthington ran a finger across his neck.

When they made it to the edge of Central Park, they hung back a moment and stared at the trees. The whole thing was incredibly impressive, reminding her of St James's Park in London—an area in the heart of the bustling city where nature was allowed to thrive.

"Jennie, look."

Jennie followed Worthington's finger toward the edge of the park, where the trees cast a shadow over the streets. It was past midnight now, a time when the clubs and bars would be heaving.

This side of the city was incredibly quiet—except for the huddle of five hooded figures nearing the gate into the park.

The head honcho, a man with wide shoulders and a wiry beard poking out of his hood, looked cautiously around to check that they weren't being followed before they disappeared underneath the canopy of trees.

Jennie caught a glint of gold around the head honcho's neck. "That's them."

"Are we sure?" Worthington asked.

Jennie smiled. "Trust me on this."

He gave her that look again. "Like that time I trusted your promise that I wouldn't be able to be sucked up by a vacuum cleaner?"

"How was I supposed to know Dysons work on spectral beings?" Jennie gave the group a few moments before running across the road and ducking behind the trees. If she stayed off the path, she could remain in the shadows.

She craned around the trunk to keep an eye on them. "Keep close," she muttered

"I live to serve," Worthington replied dryly.

The park was nearly empty except for a few late-night dog walkers and some rather brave joggers. Only occasionally did they have to duck out of sight of the group who strolled through the park as though they owned the place. They spoke, but she couldn't catch their words.

"Where are they going?" Worthington asked.

Jennie shrugged. "Back home, I guess."

"Really?"

Jennie scoffed. "Of course not."

Worthington shook his head. "You could answer me seriously for once. You're going to give a guy trust issues."

Jennie kept her eyes concentrated on the group ahead. "I can't help it. I'm a natural-born liar. Lies live in my blood. Try me; ask me what star sign I am."

"What star sign are you?" he asked wearily.

"Aries."

"Really?"

Jennie grinned. "Nope, Capricorn."

Worthington narrowed his eyes. "That was going to be my next guess."

"Well, I lied again. I'm a Cancer. See? Now you have no idea where you stand."

Worthington sighed. "I never do."

"Do you even stand?"

"Of course, I do," he replied. "I'm standing right now."

Jennie broke her stare from the group and looked at Worthington's feet. "Strange. I always thought you just kind of bobbed along."

Worthington ran a hand over his face.

"Quick, they're moving out of sight," Jennie hissed.

They ran ahead, keeping low and tight to the trees. As they crested a small rise on the park green they slowed down, realizing that the group had stopped.

There were more of them now. At least a dozen gathered around a large boulder that was as black as onyx. As the group Jennie had been following approached, the others bowed their heads and put their hands together.

The larger group mimicked the greeting. The one Jennie had identified as their leader stepped forward and waited in front of a woman wearing a blood-red robe. The color looked deep crimson in the shadows.

"Rico, at last," the woman crooned, her voice deep and sensual. Her words dripped from her tongue like hot caramel off a spoon. "I was worried you'd keep us waiting, or worse, not arrive."

"We came as fast as we could, Spirit Mother," Rico replied. "We didn't want to draw any unnecessary attention to ourselves on our way here. The city's eyes are always open."

The Spirit Mother nodded.

Jennie imagined the name was an honorific because the woman hardly seemed old enough to be the mother of a toddler.

A smaller cloaked figure stepped forward, their body so shrouded Jennie couldn't tell whether they were a man or woman. "Please, Spirit Mother. It is nearly time." They pointed to the sky where the moon was at its zenith.

A full moon ritual? How cliché.

"Lupe is right," the Spirit Mother said. "Everyone, into position. We await Lupe's signal, and then the ritual can begin at last."

They waited in tentative silence as clouds floated by, catching the silver moon's rays. Somewhere nearby, an owl hooted.

"Isn't this the part where you stop the ritual?" Worthington whispered. "Bust out your gun and go all badass on them?"

"The Big Bitch," Jennie told him distractedly.

"Excuse me?"

Jennie nodded to her hip. "She's called the 'Big Bitch.'"

"Oh." Worthington chuckled. "I get it. 'BB,' as in BB gun?"

Jennie looked at Worthington and shook her head. "No. 'Big Bitch' as in, 'if you mock my gun again, the Big Bitch is going to blow your face off.'"

Worthington gulped. "Roger that."

Jennie watched the group through narrowed eyes. She had learned over the years that it was better to understand the motives of a cult before you got involved and blew them out of the water. For all she knew, these were desperate nobodies seeking to cast magic that was beyond their ability to control.

"It is time," Lupe's voice croaked.

The Spirit Mother lowered her hood, revealing a woman so beautiful that for a fleeting moment, Jennie considered crossing over to the opposite team to spend one night with her. Her hair was the deepest black, her face pale, with lips so red they could have been made entirely of blood.

The Spirit Mother closed her eyes and held out her arms. Each member of the group followed suit until they formed a ring around the boulder.

The Spirit Mother began to hum. Beside her, Lupe began to mutter words in a tongue so ancient that Jennie couldn't recognize it. It had the familiarity of Latin, but the guttural sounds had a twist she'd never heard.

At first, nothing happened, then something began to glow within the boulder. A white-hot light emanated from inside it, as though a fire burned in the center of the rock.

"May the spirits of old, from tombs long gone cold, arise,

arise, arise!" The Spirit Mother's voice sounded faraway, as though someone else was talking through her. Someone in the depths of a well. She spoke over Lupe, raising her arms as the glow within the boulder grew.

A faint shimmer of blue uncoiled from Lupe's chest and extended outward.

"May the ghouls that were slain come alive again, arise, arise, arise!"

"Catchy tune, isn't it?" Jennie muttered. "Think it could make the iTunes top twenty?"

Worthington's nose wrinkled. "I've stopped paying attention to that chart nonsense ever since the Beatles left the scene."

"You know who gave them the idea for *Yellow Submarine*, right?" Jennie pointed her thumbs at herself.

Worthington scoffed. "Bullshit."

"Nope. Bumped into Lennon and McCartney in the Lamb & Flag, and they told me they were struggling with a song title. We joked about songs with simple names, and McCartney suggested a color and a vehicle. Luckily, I convinced them to go with *Yellow Submarine*. If it had been left up to them, they would've chosen Blue Blimp."

The rock flared, and beams of light pulsed from the center.

Worthington groaned, his eyes fixed on the boulder. "Oh, no. I've got a bad feeling about this."

"What are they doing?" Jennie muttered.

The light continued to grow as the group repeated the Spirit Mother's words in a unified chant. The coil of blue light connected from the small, hooded figure of Lupe to the center.

From their hiding place, they could now make out individual figures floating inside the boulder. The light shone through the translucent skin of their pre-natal home. They looked like tadpoles inside an egg to Jennie.

Lupe's voice reached a crescendo, accompanied by a final chorus of "Arise, arise, arise!" The Spirit Mother's arms dropped, which broke the circle. The boulder fractured, splitting into large chunks, and light exploded in a column, reaching from the broken boulder to the sky.

For a moment, Jennie could see the people in perfect color as the light illuminated the group staring open-mouthed at their creation. Several of them turned, afraid that the light would give away their position. That anyone within the park would suddenly know where they were.

Which would be true, Jennie thought, *if the light was on this plane of existence.*

The light escalated to a final blinding glare, then vanished into nothing. The group was left standing in silence.

"Did…did it work?" Rico asked.

The Spirit Mother turned to Lupe. "Well? Did it?"

Jennie nodded silently. In the center of the circle stood two spirits, a man and a woman. The woman examined her hands and legs as if she couldn't believe what she was seeing.

The man was small. He wore an old-fashioned pinstripe suit that looked as though it had been lifted straight out of a seventies gangster movie. His two-tone shoes were immaculate, as was the Tommy gun he held. "I can't believe it!" He laughed. "I'm free. Dear God, Jesus, and all that is good and holy, I'm free!"

"What does this mean?" The woman held her hands in front of her face, then patted down her frilly white dress. A dark crimson line stretched from one side of her throat to the other. Her words were laced with a strong Virginia accent. "This cannot be true."

"Truer than the dirt you're standing on." The man laughed again and took a deep sniff of the night air. "Ah, can you smell that? Freedom. Sweet, unadulterated freedom. Now to work out where we are."

"And *when* we are," Frock added.

"*Did it work?*" the Spirit Mother hissed. She looked straight through the spirits on the other side of the circle. "Did it? *Lupe, answer me!*"

The lady in the frock snorted. "What's her problem?"

"She's the one who wanted to summon us, clearly," Pinstripe told her. He strode toward the Spirit Mother and waved a hand in front of her face. "Strange. I always thought the person who summoned us would be able to at least acknowledge our existence." He turned back with a devilish grin. "Oh, the fun we can have with this."

"Fun? You think we're going to have fun?" Frock replied. "I've been trapped in the in-between for two hundred years, and you think I've broken free to come out and have some fun?"

Pinstripe gave her an incredulous look. "You don't get sarcasm, do you?"

"The lowest form of wit."

Lupe stepped forward, arms spread wide, his face still hidden by his hood. "Friends," he intoned in a thick Latino accent, "it is with the greatest pleasure that I see you reborn into our modern times."

The Spirit Mother looked from Lupe to the empty space where he was speaking with a smile on her face and confusion in her eyes.

Pinstripe approached Lupe. Both were small, but Lupe was smaller. "*You* summoned us? Well, I suppose there ought to be a thank you there." He shifted his gun to the other hand and offered a hand to Lupe.

Lupe ignored the gesture, his dark eyes glinting beneath his hood. There was a trace of a leer in the shadows that hid his face.

"Excuse me, sir, but I have a question for you," Frock told him. "What's a strange-looking man like you doing awakening spirits in the middle of the night? I mean, we sure are thankful, but you gotta admit, it doesn't make a whole lot of sense."

"Yeah," Pinstripe added. "I mean, not to cut this short or nothing, but I gots me a place to be." He opened up his jacket pocket to reveal a hole where his heart should have been, crimson stains flowering around the point of impact. "Revenge is a dish best served cold, right? I'm sure Jonny De Marco has kids around here somewhere I can really fuck up. Maybe *he's* still alive, and I can finally watch *his* heart stop ticking. Who knows?"

Lupe reached for his hood and lowered it slowly.

Frock recoiled at the sight of what lay beneath.

The man's face was a map of scars. His hair was cornrowed, and his eyes held the milky glaze of blindness. Dotted inside his mouth were gold teeth, and a wiry beard twisted down his chin.

"You're not going anywhere," Lupe replied flatly. He held his hands in front of his face, touching the thumb and forefingers of both hands together to create a diamond. As he started chanting, the rest of the group fell obediently into the chorus, and the Spirit Mother's eyes grew wide with excitement.

"Fuck this," Pinstripe told Lupe, making to leave the circle. He reached its edge and was about to pass through a small gap between two of the hooded chanters when a blinding flash of light threw him backward. "What the..."

Frock's hand went to her mouth. "Dear, are you okay?"

He looked at her in horror. "I can't...I can't get free..."

Lupe leered. The blue trail that had connected to the rock now reached out and connected to the two specters. "You thought it would be that simple? That I would release you and let you go without any recompense? You are bound to me."

The Spirit Mother looked uncertainly at Lupe. "To you? Shouldn't they be swearing to *us*? *We're* the Spectral Plane, not you."

Lupe laughed darkly, ignoring her comments.

"You think we've waited in that chunk of rock for decades so we could be released and serve a magician with an ego complex?" Pinstripe asked. "Forget it. You can't keep us contained forever."

Lupe's face soured, his brow creasing. He concentrated his energy on the pair, the cords connecting them growing thicker with each passing second. Whatever power was in him was draining the energy from the specters.

"What are you doing?" the Spirit Mother asked, clearly agitated. "Enough of this shit." She shoved Lupe and sent him sprawling to the ground.

For the briefest of moments, his power weakened.

Jennie got to her feet. "I think that's our cue."

The Spirit Mother loomed over Lupe. "We made a deal, Lupe—your powers in exchange for a place in our organization. You promised us specters, so get your shit together and deliver."

Lupe got clumsily back to his feet, re-establishing his connection with Pinstripe and Frock just as they were about to break free.

"You delivered on your part," Lupe growled. "But the prizes are *mine!*" His voice rose as he punched the Spirit Mother in the face and reached for a small pistol hidden beneath the cloak.

He fired, taking out some of the group before Jennie pulled out her pistol and shot him.

She only needed one bullet to achieve her goal. The bullet ripped through his arm and forced him to drop the gun. He looked for the location of his attacker, his eyes widening hungrily as he saw Worthington trailing behind her.

Pinstripe and Frock used the distraction to flee from the circle. They moved fast, shooting into the trees.

Jennie fired another shot at his feet—a final warning shot. This time he grinned as he concentrated his powers on the spirits now disappearing from sight, and a final tendril of power shot out from him, latched itself onto Pinstripe and pulled him back to the group at an impressive speed.

Jennie thought about running after him but stopped when several of the surviving group aimed pistols at her head.

She turned slowly, looking each gang member in the eye. Their hands shook, their guns aimed more out of fear than anger. "In case you didn't notice, *I'm* the one who just saved all your arses," she told them angrily. "So put down your guns before I find a way to do it for you."

The Spirit Mother lowered her gun and signaled for the others to do the same. They obeyed reluctantly, still unsure what had just happened.

"Thank you for saving us," she told Jennie, begrudging every word.

"Not a problem," Jennie replied, eyeing the Spirit Mother closely. Now that she was closer, she could see the gold chain around her neck, its pendant tucked neatly into the cleavage of her clothing. "Let me guess. You guys are the Spectral Plane?"

The Spirit Mother nodded.

Jennie frowned. "Great. Then we've got a lot to discuss. Not the least of which is what the fuck happened here tonight."

CHAPTER SIX

<u>Midtown Manhattan, New York City, Present Day</u>

"I've known for as long as I can remember that something lay beyond the great veil," the Spirit Mother told Jennie. There was frenzied excitement in her voice as she traced a finger over a shelf packed with books. "Ever since I was a little girl and my mother died, I knew there was more to life than death."

Jennie and Worthington sat side by side on a couch that looked a lot more comfortable than it was. The headquarters of the Spectral Plane was nothing more than a run-down rental unit on the south side of Manhattan. Several outdated rooms in need of a good lick of paint and a clean.

"Hardly the headquarters of a thriving organization," Jennie whispered to Worthington as they walked through the door and saw members of the cult sitting in the rooms or lying on the floors asleep. "Looks more like a drug den to me."

While Worthington kept trying to catch her eye, Jennie ignored him. It wouldn't be right to reveal she had her very own specter sitting beside her right now.

Jennie smiled gently. "What happened to her, Spirit Mother?"

"Please, call me Tanya," the Spirit Mother replied. "She was killed in a hit and run, murdered by a guy whose blood was more alcohol than plasma. Ah!" She pulled a book from the shelf and flicked through the pages.

She carried on her story, tongue poking out the side of her mouth intermittently. "It was a lot to take for a five-year-old girl, but time heals all wounds. That didn't mean that I didn't...*feel* her after she had gone."

"I'm sorry for your loss." Jennie meant every word.

Tanya waved a hand. "That was years ago."

Jennie nodded. "So, at what point did you begin to believe in ghosts?"

"Around the time she visited me in the middle of the night," Tanya replied. "It was a few days after the funeral. My father kept the curtains open and told me that Mom would watch me from heaven. I couldn't sleep that night. Don't ask me why. I guess a thousand thoughts pass through a child's brain when their parent dies at such a young age. I felt something at the edge of my bed and peeked out of the covers to see a shimmer of *something* there."

"A shimmer?" Worthington scoffed. "How cliché."

Jennie shot him a look, thankful that Tanya couldn't hear his words.

"And you think it was your mum?" Jennie asked.

"I *know* it was her," Tanya replied. "She'd come to say a final goodbye. To check on her baby. Ever since then, I've made it my mission to seek out books, texts, artifacts—*anything* that'll bring me one step closer to unveiling the truth to the beyond and seeing another spirit in real life."

Jennie had heard similar tales down the years.

"Here," Tanya exclaimed. She crossed the room excitedly and took a seat in the spot where Worthington was sitting.

Worthington recoiled, throwing his arms in the air as if receiving a very unwelcome lap dance.

Tanya shivered, but otherwise, she seemed not to notice. "*The Turn of the Screw*, written in 1898. Look at this." She traced a finger along a line so highlighted and annotated that the original text was barely noticeable. "*I seemed to float not into clearness, but into a darker obscure, and within a minute there had come to me out of my very pity the appalling alarm of his perhaps being innocent.* He's talking about ghosts."

"Yes, well, Henry James was always something of a crackpot," Jennie replied. "The ego went to his head after that book. Big theater goer, though, which I never understood. Sussex to London at that time of the world was a bitch of a commute."

Tanya raised an eyebrow. "You talk as if you knew him."

Jennie cast her eyes to the floor. "History major. I geek out about biographies and origin stories."

Tanya hesitated a moment before returning to the bookshelf and retrieving a handful more books. "They're all here. All the accounts of ghosts and stories I tracked down of what lies in the afterlife. Look." As she retrieved quotes from dog-eared pages, she slapped the books and threw them to the floor.

She read from Christina Dodd.

"So, you know you're a ghost?"
　　I looked at my hands; they were transparent and glowed faintly.
　　"Can you think of another explanation?"

Mark Ristau:

"Very soon you will find yourself at the end of a dirt road, only inches from a threshold...a threshold into another world—a glorious world, one of infinite possibilities. You'll be standing there contemplating your next move when a gust of wind whispers, "Have faith." When you hear those magic words, it'll be time for you to cross the threshold and begin your journey..."

S. Vest:

"As the years passed, it became clear that Alio was a ghost, not an imaginary friend. Imaginary friends have no borders, but ghosts often do."

And more.

It soon became clear that Tanya's entire library was a collection of selected works of fiction and non-fiction centered around the theme of ghosts and sightings of the supernatural. She stood to fetch yet more books but Jennie called her back, saying she'd seen enough.

Tanya blushed as she sat back on the couch.

Worthington recoiled again. "She must be a riot at dinner parties," he deadpanned.

Jennie fought back a laugh.

"You must think I'm crazy," Tanya told her. "There are many people who do."

"Not your buddies in the Spectral Plane, I imagine?" Jennie replied. "They seem to be on your side."

"All except that traitor Lupe," Tanya growled, placing her head in her hands. "We were so damn close. I could *feel* it."

Jennie saw her chance. "Close to what? What were you guys doing out there? What was that out in the park?"

Tanya took a deep breath through clenched teeth. "Lupe was one of the newest members of our organization. I've spent the last six months tracking down ancient artifacts in New York that have been rumored to have been connected with spectral poltergeist activity." She gave an appreciable grin. "You wouldn't believe how many ghost stories there are in a city that has only been around for a few hundred years."

Jennie would.

"During that time, I've seen everything from…" She made air quotes. "A haunted kettle to a possessed chihuahua. Suffice to say that my energy for searching grew less over time, and although I had the support of several others I'd met along the way who showed an interest in the afterlife, I was beginning to lose steam."

Jennie nodded. "Understandable."

Worthington shifted out from under Tanya. "I bet the kettle didn't run out of steam."

"But then I got a phone call from an anonymous source telling me there had been a spike in spectral activity in the city. There were even a few clippings of hospitals reporting strange activity in their wards, a spate of terminally ill patients muttering unintelligibly about swearing their allegiances to people before they died."

Tanya crossed the room and picked up a battered folder, which she dropped on the table in front of Jennie. The laminated sleeves inside were filled with press clippings of black and white pictures of hospital fronts and baffled doctors. Some showed men and women with unkempt hair pointing at telephones and TV remotes that were clearly held up by a string for photographic effect.

Jennie leaned forward, flattening a sheet of paper that showed a headline saying, "*Who ya gonna call?*"

Worthington rolled his eyes. "Really? A *Ghostbusters* joke? Do they not have any other frame of reference? *The Others? Poltergeist? The Haunting of Hill House?*"

"When was this?" Jennie asked, unable to take her eyes off the clippings as she flicked from page to page.

"A month or so ago," Tanya replied. "It's still happening now. I get a phone call a couple of times a day reporting ghost sightings, and I head over to investigate. My name has made something of an impact since I'm always one of the first to check out the scene."

"Before the pigs?" Jennie asked.

Tanya arched an eyebrow. "Pigs?"

"You know. The coppers?"

Tanya shook her head. "What are you talking about?"

"The 'Ol' Bill?' Boys in blue? Bobbies?"

Worthington leaned through Tanya to Jennie. "She's a Yank, remember?"

Tanya shook her head again. "Nope. Nothing."

Jennie laughed, the realization suddenly dawning on her. "I mean the police."

"Oh, the cops?" Tanya chuckled.

"Right," Jennie replied. "You get to the scene of the crime before they do?"

Tanya chuckled. "Oh, easily. The cops don't give two flying fucks about some mama's boy in his parents' basement proclaiming that his can of Monster has flown off his table and onto the floor, or that his TV turned from crystal clarity to a pile of fuzzy static. They're off solving real crimes. You know, murders and drug deals and rapes. That kind of thing."

Jennie thought back to the drug deals she'd seen going on in alleys around New York. She thought of the brutal beating the homeless man was subjected to. "They're not doing a great job," she muttered.

"What was that?"

Jennie waved a hand. "So, this spike in reports began around a month ago? How does Lupe tie into all of this?"

Tanya sighed. "Lupe was going to be the key to unlocking it all, I was sure of it. He turned up one day after I was done investigating at an apartment in Manhattan. An old woman thought her dog had been possessed; turned out to be a bad case of an overly enthusiastic pup. Anyway, as I was leaving the apartment, Lupe was waiting for me in the street. At first, I thought he was another loony trying to get me to speak to one of his long-lost loved ones, but then he told me that he had the gift of being able to see the specters."

"And you believed him?"

"Of course," Tanya replied without a shadow of a doubt. "Why wouldn't I?"

Jennie looked at Worthington for help.

"What are you looking at me for?" he asked. "She can't see me, remember? If she chooses to be bat-shit insane, that's for you to deal with."

Jennie shook her head. "Please continue."

"He took me back to his apartment and showed me things. Sketches, pictures, items he'd gathered over the years to help him commune with the deceased." A small smile grew on Tanya's face. "Their presence was so strong. For the first time in my life, it was like I was sitting next to something I've been searching so long for."

Worthington put an ethereal hand on Tanya's leg and placed his face millimeters from hers. In a voice louder than necessary, he said, "I guess we can rule you out of having the gift, then!"

Jennie bit her lip to stop herself from laughing.

Tanya didn't seem to notice, lost in the memories in her head. "For the next few hours, we talked and talked, and he told me about all the experiences he'd had. He told me he could *see* specters all around the city. Told me he had a way to call them over to our side and have them work with us. Promised me answers to the questions we've had since time began."

"And how did he propose to do that?" Jennie asked.

For the first time since they had entered the organization's headquarters, a flicker of shame darkened Tanya's face. Her eyes danced from Jennie to the floor. "Through oaths."

Jennie's heart rate quickened, the whole ordeal going from jovial to serious in the flick of a switch. She knew the power oaths had over the mortal after they crossed to the spectral side of the veil. The entirety of Queen Victoria's reign as the head of the paranormal court was centered around the loyalties and oaths that were sworn to the crown during the first moments after a person chose to remain on Earth as a specter.

It was how Worthington had become a specter under the queen's rule. It was how all of Jennie's former specter companions had found themselves under the rule of the paranormal queen. Darwin, Alessia, Hubert, Katrina, and all the specters who came before them, they had all said the sacred words that bound them to the crown and plunged them into the service of the paranormal court.

Not that anyone minded. For those who knew what was to come, it was an honor and a privilege to have the opportunity to continue their service to the crown. Those who didn't believe in the afterlife found themselves pleasantly surprised to be serving the power who ruled the paranormal world.

Yet, these oaths couldn't have been to the crown. Queen Victoria had stated that there had been an unruly rising in disloyal specters rising in New York City, a whole city going out of control and threatening to revolt against her rule over America.

So, what the hell were these oaths?

Jennie shifted in her chair and met Tanya's eyes. "You say that like you're ashamed. What did you do?"

Tanya took a steadying breath. "Lupe took us to the hospitals and hospices across the city and somehow faked his way into visiting those who were within inches of their death. As they lay there gasping in their final moments of mortality, he promised them a better life, a life in which they could still visit their loved ones and watch them grow old." She looked at the ceiling. "He promised them things. So many things."

Jennie placed a hand on Tanya's arm. "What was promised? Who did they swear to?"

"They swore to *him*. They swore to Lupe, and then they passed."

She told Jennie about the number of promises that were made. The hundreds of dying souls promised a life in the ever after.

"How many of these specters now serve under Lupe's command?" Jennie asked.

Tanya shrugged, deflated. "How am I supposed to know? None? All of them? I can't see ghosts, remember? I just had to trust what he told me and hope that something came to fruition. Call me crazy—"

"Bitch is crazy," Worthington muttered.

"But I really thought that he was the real deal." She nodded her head slightly. "I suppose tonight proves that in some way, he was."

Jennie cast her mind back to the events at Central Park. The boulder of obsidian splitting as light spilled from within. The birth of two specters who had found themselves trapped in the rock. It was something that she had never come across in all of her nearly hundred and forty years of life. "What did happen tonight? What were you doing in the park?"

Worthington finally sat forward, taking an interest.

"It was our last shot with Lupe," Tanya explained. "After several months of activity which I grew increasingly uncomfortable with—the Spectral Plane is meant to *serve* the people to find answers, not give them false hope and promises for an afterlife we'd never see—it all came together for the last effort before we kicked Lupe from the group. He knew about my fascination for artifacts and stumbled across some work I had been doing a few years ago in the city. See, when New York was founded in 1624, it was nothing more than a landmass waiting to accommodate a civilization. Over the years since its creation, there have been a number of…shall we say, *interesting* incidents that have suggested that magic might have once existed. Curses, burials, rituals, a great number of these have been enacted upon the living and the dead, and there is a wealth of evidence which suggests that *some* spirits may have actually found themselves trapped within certain natural materials which can be found across the city."

"You're saying that black magic has encased spirits in objects?" The idea sounded ludicrous to Jennie, but how else could tonight be explained?

"Think about it." The keen glint in Tanya's eye returned. "New York was founded in 1624. Sixty-eight years later, the witch trials in Salem began. I don't think it's a coincidence that our forebears believed in powers beyond humanity."

Jennie saw the issue with what Tanya was telling her. "If what you're saying is true, wouldn't that mean the spirits encased in these items would be corrupt? Maybe even evil?"

Tanya blushed again. "It was worth the risk."

Jennie got to her feet, feeling a sudden need to move. Often, she found walking around helped her clear her head and process her thoughts. She stood by the window and peeked through the blinds. Morning was making its way over the city, the purples and blacks of the night sky replaced by a soft pink glow.

"We need to find Lupe, and we need to find these specters," Jennie decided, looking at Worthington.

Tanya followed Jennie's gaze into emptiness and moved her head to meet her eyes.

Worthington scoffed.

"You believe me?" she asked, amazed.

Jennie nodded. "Despite how ludicrous other people might think you sound, you'll be surprised to know that I have a large amount of experience in the arena we're dealing with here."

Tanya's eyes widened.

Jennie nodded. "Yep. Spirits are real, life beyond death is real, and your good buddy Lupe has upset the balance and unleashed hundreds of non-aligned specters into a city that has been under the rule of Our Paranormal Majesty for over a century. You're an accomplice to this, but you're also an innocent, so you're forgiven."

A strange noise came from Tanya's mouth as it flapped open and closed. She was stunned.

"Oh, and that cold chill you might be feeling? You're currently sitting on a specter."

Tanya jumped up so suddenly it was as though she'd been

electrocuted. She stared at the sofa where Worthington was waving at her, unable to see him. She reached forward and waved her arm back and forth through his face, able to feel the slightest change in temperature.

Worthington sighed. "If only I could reach out and slap *her*. Do you realize how demeaning this is?"

Jennie laughed.

"Oh, wow. You're serious!" Tanya repeated the action, a frenzied excitement taking over. "Who is it? What's their name? Can they see me right now?"

Worthington sat back grumpily and folded his arms.

"There's no time for that." Jennie chuckled. "I need you to tell me everything you can about that boulder and Lupe and give me any possible leads on where that freak lives." Her face grew serious. "We've got a specter to catch."

Tanya's face straightened. "Okay, but if I tell you all this, promise me you'll introduce me to your friend."

Jennie rolled her eyes. "I'll try, but I should let you know in advance, he's rather shy."

Worthington stuck his middle finger up.

CHAPTER SEVEN

<u>New York City, USA, Present Day</u>

Baxter roamed the darkened streets of the city with his socket wrench balanced over one shoulder and his other hand nestled safely in his pocket.

He liked this time of night, the early hours before morning. When the city was at its sleepiest, and even the scumbags of the city had tucked themselves away for fear of early-morning encounters with the cops.

It was a time when a man could breathe the air and appreciate having a life after death. Being able to roam in relative safety, knowing humans couldn't see him, and the worst your fellow specters would do is give you the stink-eye and go down the next street.

Or at least, that was the way it had been until very recently.

"Recently" being a relative term for a specter who had spent the better part of thirty years in the city and nearly a hundred years in the afterlife.

Things had become unsettled; even he could feel that. Sure, there were always fanatics who tried to force you to submit to the crown and swear your allegiance, but they always gave up in the end. The queen might hold a firm grip on Europe, but her power had a lesser influence on this side of the Pond.

But now there were whispers of a second faction, and specters he'd come to know well were choosing to take a rebellious stance instead of the neutral one many had adopted over the years.

A stance *he* had adopted.

Man, just when you think that the afterlife is going to be peaceful...

Baxter turned onto Seventh Avenue and let the sounds of the sleepy city wash over him. Somewhere nearby, a creature was rustling in the trash-laden alley behind the movie theater. In the nearby apartments came the frantic grunts of a man reaching climax. A few cabs drove lazily by, looking for the late-night custom that came from last-calls and kick-outs in the city's nightclubs.

Peace was hard to come by these days, especially when your own kind were starting to turn on each other like hungry jackals. Fear made people make crazy choices.

As he strolled down the street toward Radio City Music Hall, he found his mind wandering to the woman and the specter he had met earlier that night.

He had never seen anyone like her. A human who could communicate and talk to specters, of all people!

He closed his eyes and pictured the scene. Remembered the expression on her face as she took down the thugs who'd attacked her. Not a smidgen of fear in her eyes. Not a shudder of hesitation as she took their asses and handed them back on a silver platter.

And to have lifted them, too.

Yes, indeed, there was something about that woman that had his attention, not least the tricksy little weapon holstered to her side.

Not the pistol, no. That kind of shit he'd seen countless times over the years. The Glock was a staple of modern society, something seen in more often Americans' pockets than TicTacs.

It was the other gun. That one piqued the part of his brain that strived to understand. To *know* how things worked and examine the cogs and gears that made them function. The gun was unlike anything he had seen before. Easy enough for the untrained eye to mistake for a sawed-off shotgun, but there was something different about it. Something…

Custom.

Saying the word made him shiver with excitement in much the same way experimenting on that 1905 De Dietrich automobile had filled him with such unbridled wonder that he had gotten overenthusiastic with the gasoline and been blown skyward in the resulting massive explosion.

Not a great way to go.

He had to know more. He had to find out more about this woman and the weapon she owned. Learn about the talents she possessed and discover where her gifts came from. If he didn't, he knew there'd always be that tiny part of him left hollow. Left to wonder if there was something he could have done to learn about that weapon.

And it's not like he didn't have all the time in the world to do it.

Well, unless he found himself on the business end of an exorcism.

Baxter gave an amused snort and turned down Forty-Ninth Street, alone in his own little world, until someone called out from behind him.

"Oi, big guy. We need a word."

Baxter turned to see the brutish woman and her entourage from earlier that evening approaching. Baxter felt his hackles raise but remained calm. He was surprised to see that the lower half of her face had already recovered. Two pale lips protruded from the stump of her face.

"You've not said enough already tonight?" he asked.

The woman gave a derisive laugh. She was being guided along by two of her companions, led like a blind woman.

Which was accurate, considering half her head had been blown off.

"I expected a big guy to have a big mouth. Tell me, big guy, where did you find your little mortal companion? She caused quite a stir tonight, didn't she?"

They closed in on him, the brutes circling him close. The woman's face was an absolute mess. The only part of her face that worked was the mouth, and even so, her words lacked clarity.

"At least I have my whole head." Baxter smirked. "Come on, sweetheart; you really need to feel more pain tonight?"

The woman chuckled, the sound like bubbling oil. "No one needs to feel any pain, darling. We just wanna know where you met the girl, and where we can find her. Our contact is very curious to meet the mortal who can talk to the specters."

Baxter shrugged. "I can't help you, I'm afraid. She's gone. Just met her tonight, she did her business, and she's on her way. Last I heard, she was heading down to Central Park, but that would have been a few hours ago."

Movement from behind. Baxter felt something move closer to his back.

Or someone.

He reached for his hat and doffed it. "If that's all you've got to say, I'll be on my way."

"Get him!"

Baxter knew what was coming before it even happened.

The brute who had moved directly behind him hooked an arm around Baxter's body and went for his throat.

Baxter ducked swiftly so the brute only got him around the chest and kicked backward off the ground as hard as he could. His weight toppled the specter to the sidewalk, where he became a convenient cushion to soften Baxter's landing. He rolled sideways off the brute and got to his feet, immediately drawing his revolver.

He took a breath, pausing for a second to let the shock of the landing subside. Although the real-world pains he had experienced in his years of living—and in that fateful moment before death—were far worse than what he felt as a specter, being shot or stabbed as a ghost left its mark, and would be more than uncomfortable.

Check exhibit A, he thought as he aimed the revolver at the woman.

"What's happening?" she screamed, whirling blindly. "Where is he? Get him!"

The two specters came from either side of Baxter. While he was hardly a small specimen of a man, the other two were larger.

The one on his left threw a mean left hook and caught Baxter's cheek, while the other wrestled the revolver from his hand. He bent Baxter's thumb back, and the weapon clattered to the ground as he twisted his arm behind his back.

"Aw, poor baby," the specter mocked. "Guess you'll be shooting blanks during this fight."

Baxter struggled against his grip, the right side of his face throbbing. When the brute who punched him came in for another blow, he ducked his head out of his path and head-butted the one holding him square in the nose.

The one holding his arm squeezed tighter in retaliation.

Baxter reached into his pocket with his free hand and withdrew a tiny golden ball covered in intricate etchings. There was a small nodule on the top, which he pressed as he shoved the item into the center of his captor's chest. "Here, bozo. Try this one on for size."

The specter looked down in amazement as legs grew from the orb and gripped his skin. A stream of thick gas blew out of the top of the ball, smothering him instantly in a thick fog that forced him to cough and release his grip.

Baxter took the opportunity to kick the asshole in the knee and he buckled to the ground. Baxter grinned in satisfaction at his little invention before he became aware of someone coming at him.

He had no time to turn before two powerful arms wrapped around his chest and dragged him backward. He was slammed into the wall and subjected to the pummeling of fists against his stomach.

From a few meters away, the specter Baxter had head-butted stood shakily on his damaged leg, his hand clamped to his temple. He looked around dazedly, trying to find Baxter. When he saw his comrade attacking the inventor by the wall, he began limping over.

Great puffs of air were forced out of Baxter's stomach until there was virtually nothing left. He closed his eyes, this time reaching into his other pocket, from which he withdrew a number of small black pills.

Between blows, Baxter managed to shove the pills into his attacker's mouth. His attack lessened momentarily as the specter made to spit the pills out. Baxter gave a quick upward slap to his jaw and forced the pills to the back of his throat, and a quick two-fingered jab to the specter's Adam's apple forced him to swallow.

Then the pills were gone.

The brute took a step back and clutched his throat. "What the hell?"

"Some pills are bitter to swallow, eh?" Baxter wheezed as he refilled his lungs. "Especially when those are filled with sodium, an element better known for being explosive when it comes into contact with water."

The specter's eyes widened.

Baxter grinned. "Yeah, give it a few seconds for your body to dissolve the safety film. You'll feel a little sore in the morning."

The specter doubled over and stuck his fingers down his

throat. He began dry-heaving, trying his best to cough the pills back up.

"High school flashbacks," Baxter muttered, realizing suddenly that the other specter's knee had recovered and he was picking up speed as he came for him. He saw his socket wrench lying on the ground and dodged around the specter doing his best to empty his stomach.

"Okay, enough of my flashy tricks." Baxter scooped up the wrench and held it like a baseball bat. *What are we thinking, Bax? Home run?*

The specter coming for Baxter kept his eyes focused on him. He had no awareness whatsoever of Baxter's weapon.

Baxter swung the wrench in a full arc, and the metal connected with the asshole's skull.

The specter was thrown to the side, where he collided with a nearby mailbox and dropped to the ground in a heavy snooze.

Baxter nodded smugly. "Still got it." He walked past the cloud of smoke and back toward the woman who had sent her dogs to attack him.

She knelt on the ground, hands grasped as if in prayer. "Please don't hurt me. I can't take any more pain…"

Baxter moved to one knee, staring at where her eyes used to be. "Funny, isn't it? When we died, we thought we'd escaped it all. We thought, 'Hey, you know what we'll never experience again? Love. Pain. Hot. Cold. All that shit.' Yet, here we are. You, a festering pile of dog shit, and me with bruised ribs and a headache that could kill a horse."

"Please," the woman gasped between continued sobs.

Baxter would have felt sorry for her if she hadn't brought the situation on herself. "The thing is, I like my afterlife easy. I like a cloudless day and a stroll by the Hudson. When shit starts getting in the way of that, I find myself irked. Have you ever been irked…" He leaned closer. "This is that part where you say your name."

"Joan," she blubbered. "My name is Joan,"

Baxter nodded. "Great. Have you ever been irked, Joan?"

Joan shook her head.

"Well, it's not a great feeling," Baxter told her. "And the only way I think I'm going to be able to forgive you and let you and your men go on your merry way is if you tell me what I want to know."

Joan sniveled, which seemed impossible given that her nose was mincemeat. "What's that?"

Baxter smiled as if it was obvious. "I want you to tell me who the fuck sent you, and why the hell you're so hellbent on fucking up the representatives of the Winter Court."

CHAPTER EIGHT

Midtown Manhattan, New York City, Present Day

Plates littered the table in front of Jennie, the bone-white china stained yellow and brown with grease. In her hands was the final half of the New Yorker deluxe burger—the third she'd managed to work her way through—but she hardly felt full.

"You know," Jennie told Worthington, picking a chunk of beef from between her teeth with the nail of her little finger. "As great as these burgers are, the table service here is deplorable."

Jennie nodded to the pile of plates, wondering if the busboys were too busy servicing the restaurant since they hadn't cleared her table.

Worthington's nose wrinkled. "Maybe they're waiting for you to lick the grease from each plate?" He pointed at a small chunk of beef that had broken free of the bun. "You missed a piece."

"Thanks!" Jennie mumbled through her mouthful.

She was in high spirits. Of the thousands of beds she had slept in during her life, the Plaza's offered a level of comfort that she had never felt before. She wasn't sure what thread count the sheets were, but she would try to find a supplier to provide her with the same on her return to England.

Not only that, but the hotel was *quiet*. Considering the Plaza overlooked Central Park and was located in the very center of one of the busiest metropolitan cities in the world, the room was soundproof. In fact, had it not been for Worthington tripping over his own feet and waking her up, she might have slept right through the night.

"I don't understand where your appetite comes from." Worthington's eyes were fixed on Jennie's mouth, a mixture of intrigue and disgust on his face. "You have such a skinny frame."

"You're just jealous because you can't taste food," Jennie retorted. "Here..." She leaned across the table and shoved the burger where Worthington's mouth was. The burger hovered in the space as he stared at her with a bored expression.

Across the restaurant, one of the busboys pointed to Jennie, snickering behind his hand.

Worthington heard him and turned to see what was going on. "See? Maybe that's the reason they won't approach you. You're a lunatic feeding a burger to thin air and talking to no one."

Jennie smirked. "I'm talking to you."

"They can't see that."

Jennie shrugged. "I don't care. Do you think I haven't gotten used to the strange looks and the sideways glances after living with specters since the nineteenth century? I'm long over it, my man. Maybe you should get over it, too."

Jennie finished her burger, every last morsel, and sat back with a satisfied feeling. "American food isn't bad."

"What were you expecting?" Worthington looked across the restaurant. It was getting busy—peak hour in the city. Couples walked by the restaurant in dresses and suits, many ready to head to the Theater District and catch a show. A few families tried to wrangle their energetic children, to no avail.

Jennie shrugged. "Not sure. After all the adverts and TV shows I'd seen, I was expecting everything to taste like grease and fat. Turns out, there's flavor and good meat. Maybe I'll stay here a while, except I'd get fat eating like this all the time."

A busboy came over to the table and scooped up the plates as Jennie finished her sentence. He shook his head disapprovingly, making an effort to speed up and get out of her way.

"It was a compliment," she called after him as he disappeared behind the door to the kitchen. "Well, there goes his tip."

"You *should* tip," Worthington told her. "When in Rome, and all that."

"What? What if I got shitty service and didn't want to tip?" Jennie argued.

Worthington continued to stare around the restaurant. "It's just how they do it here. If you don't like it, you can always go home."

"Oh, sure. The queen would love that. If I knocked on her door, she'd..." Jennie's voice trailed off as she wondered what *would* happen if she knocked on the queen's door and told her she'd abandoned the job because she didn't like the Americans' tipping system. She'd seen the queen angry before, but rarely at her.

She settled her bill—with a tip for the busboy—and walked through the restaurant toward the exit. As they neared the door, Jennie saw what Worthington had been staring at this whole time.

A young specter in a long and elegant gown, who'd died in her early twenties, was sitting in a booth next to a living man who looked as though life had hit him over the head repeatedly.

Jennie winked. "She's cute, huh?"

Worthington pulled his eyes away as the specter looked up from her former lover.

Jennie's hands glowed white and she shoved Worthington out of the door, the force enough for him to fly straight through the glass into the street.

"What was that for?" he complained.

"We're here on business, remember?"

Worthington gave her a sour look. "That didn't stop you from shoveling burgers down your throat until you were fit to burst, did it? I've seen pelicans eat more gracefully than you."

Jennie let the comment slide, placing her hands in her pockets as they headed out into the city.

Worthington followed her in silence, knowing that when Jennie got her mad on, it was better to leave her to her thoughts.

Now that they were out in the crowded side of New York—with patrons spilling out of bars and restaurants and celebrating the end of their workday with copious amounts of alcohol and a promise of sex—she began to notice specters here and there.

She wondered what the difference was between her life and that of a specter. Her gift had granted her long life and talents that would make any man or woman green with envy, but what was it actually like to have passed over the border into death? How different would it really be?

She walked past a specter so obese that he had to shuffle to walk and waved at him.

The specter performed a double-take and was left open-mouthed as Jennie walked on by.

Back in London, there weren't many specters who she didn't know. Considering that most who passed into death vowed their fealty to the crown, there was a constant line of new blood joining the Supernatural Court.

Since Jennie was utilized as the queen's primary agent, even if they didn't know her by look, they'd know her by name, which kept the wheels greased and kept the system working. Non-aligned specters were met by the court's Royal Recruiters and, nine times out of ten, the recently deceased would give their allegiance to the crown under the promise of a better afterlife and a helping hand when the time came to exorcise themselves into the final abyss. The darkness which lived beyond death.

Those who refused were granted a license to live in the afterlife, with the anecdote that they may only reside within the boundaries of where their mortal relatives lived.

Which sounded great, to begin with. But after watching over their own family for years, they'd begin to get bored. When their former lover decided to finally move on and shack up with the neighbor's son, they'd get angry. An angry ghost trapped in his old residence who wants only to stop or intercept any chance of romance will find himself doing nasty things within the boundaries of his powers.

The most powerful of these would become what mortals knew as "poltergeists," and what the court would label "a bloody nuisance."

A few days later, the poltergeist would be exorcised, and all that would be left of the non-aligned specter would be a hollow memory that would soon be forgotten.

Jennie crossed the street and made for the large building by the edge of the river Hudson. She waved at several cars that stopped in their tracks and honked their horns as she passed.

As she hopped onto the sidewalk outside the hospital's entrance, she wondered what became of the non-aligned in the US. The specters who were new to the world. Before they'd encountered the other specters hanging out in the underbelly of society, and before they were even aware of what the afterlife was.

Only one way to find out, she thought.

New York-Presbyterian Hospital, Lower Manhattan, Present Day

"I'm sorry, ma'am, but visiting hours are over."

Jennie removed her glasses to reveal eyes shimmering with tears.

"Please, have some compassion. My uncle...I've traveled all

the way from London to see him, and I'm worried I won't get the chance to say goodbye."

The nurse behind the reception counter looked out from under her glasses. Jennie had seen her type before-a woman so hardened from years and years of sob stories and working around the dying and the grieving that the only authority she recognized was the hospital rules.

The nurse snorted air through her nose. "What's your uncle's name?"

Jennie looked over the nurse's shoulder to where Worthington was peeking down at a logbook of visitors and a stack of patient clipboards.

"Rodriguez." He squinted at the paper. "Rogelio Rodriguez."

Jennie repeated this to the nurse, instantly regretting saying the words out loud.

"*You're* the niece of Rogelio Rodriguez?" the nurse asked skeptically.

Jennie gave her best smile. "That's right. My father and his family moved to London when I was a little girl. My mother was actually born in Leeds, so I was unlucky not to get the Latino genes." She gave a half-shrug. "Maybe my children will be blessed with my family's heritage, eh?"

The nurse stared at Jennie for a few uncomfortable seconds before slamming her clipboard shut.

"Look, Ms. um…" She took a deep breath. "*Rodriguez.* I'm sorry, but policy is policy. You can come back tomorrow morning between the hours of eight AM and twelve noon, or come back in the afternoon." She picked up the stack of clipboards and held them to her chest. "Otherwise, there's nothing I can do. Sylvia, will you please show Ms. Rodriguez the way out?"

A scrawny nurse with her hair thrown into a messy top bun nodded and scampered their way.

Jennie reluctantly obeyed, following her directions to the corridor outside of the intensive care unit.

"Straight down the elevator to the bottom floor, and straight in front of you," the scrawny nurse told her with a smile. Though she looked exhausted, it was great to see that at least one nurse in this place cared enough to show some genuine affection.

"Thank you," Jennie smiled back. "We'll be back in the morning."

"Your uncle's vitals are great. He's holding on. I'll pass him your love."

Jennie waved a sarcastic goodbye as the elevator doors shut.

"Rodriguez?" Jennie suddenly snapped at Worthington. "Out of all the names on those boards you could have gone for, *Rodriguez*? Do I look Hispanic to you?"

"I was under pressure," Worthington replied. "You try to look through clipboards without moving them and alerting the nurse to your presence."

"You know what?" Jennie rubbed a hand over her face. "Enough talking. Make yourself useful."

Before Worthington could protest, Jennie closed her eyes and began to draw power from him. She felt her body becoming immaterial, and when she opened her eyes and looked into the mirror, she could see no reflection.

"Perfect," she snarked. "If only the Army had a thousand of me for their covert ops."

"They'd struggle to get them into the tanks due to their fat heads," Worthington quipped.

He shut up the instant Jennie turned and glared at him. "One more peep out of you, and I'm shipping you first-class back to England."

"Then who will you have to bully and abuse?"

"I'm sure I'll find someone else," Jennie replied as the elevator doors opened. She stepped toward the intensive care ward. "Now shut up and keep your ears open. We've got a job to do."

The intensive care ward was as quiet as a library. The only sounds were the steady beeping of machinery tracking patients' vital organs and the occasional clop of nurses' footsteps as they trailed down the halls.

They stayed in the hospital for hours, familiarizing themselves with the layout of the building and the patients spaced out among the various single-bed rooms on the ward.

Jennie passed through curtains and hovered over the patients, staring into faces blank with unconsciousness. She examined charts and read their stories, looking to find the patients most likely to be candidates for the next life.

All of the rooms in the ward were named after plants and flowers, an attempt to veil the morbidity this ward represented.

In the Lotus Room, Jennie came across Michael Dover, a seventy-eight-year-old organ donor from Long Island who had recently suffered a heart attack. His prognosis was bleak, and Jennie knew that soon he would find himself cast into the corridor to the beyond, where he would be able to make his final choice.

In the Lavender Room, Jennie introduced herself silently to Carolyn Hurst, a twenty-four-year-old woman who had been involved in a hit and run and suffered major internal trauma. A punctured lung and several damaged organs were a lot to come back from.

And in the Lily Room, Worthington read the story of a woman in her late fifties named Betty Garland who had simply been in the wrong place at the wrong time, walking through the back streets of New York during the climax of a gang raid in which a number of store clerks were shot and killed and civilians were badly injured, Betty included.

Jennie made her rounds across the ward and found herself back at Carolyn. When she rested a hand on top of the ECG monitor, she felt the dust coat her palm and rubbed her hands together to clean them. The machine let out a few irregular beeps, then continued its pattern.

"Magical machines, aren't they?" she mused, staring at the peaceful face of the young woman. "A TV screen that can show you how your heart is beating and track any irregular activity. Einthoven really did something amazing here, didn't he?"

Worthington came over to the other side of the bed, a look of boredom on his face. "Another of your friends?"

"I wouldn't say we were friends. We attended the same cocktail party once. Not that he would remember, I was invisible at the time." Jennie shook her head. "Did you know that the first iteration of this machine was invented in 1895, but it took almost seventy years before they were commercialized and brought into modern hospitals?"

"Doesn't surprise me," Worthington replied. "Humanity has a certain amount of friction against mass manufacturing the things that might actually help its progress and development. I waited *years* for them to invent those little bone-shaped containers that attached to leads so it was easier to carry bags for dog crap, and they didn't even release them in my time!"

Jennie gave the Beefeater an incredulous look. "You've really got to sort out your priorities, Conrad."

"If you say so, Genevieve," Worthington replied stiffly.

Jennie took a seat beside Carolyn's bed. She rested her head back and closed her eyes, allowing her mind to empty.

Twenty minutes later, the ECG emitted a long, continuous flatline that woke Jennie up. She heard the sudden rush of feet and suddenly realized she'd lost her connection to Worthington and was now visible.

In a matter of seconds, she rectified the problem, but not before the first nurse arrived on the scene.

"Paddles, Diane!" The stickler for the rules who had kicked them out of the hospital earlier snapped. "What are you waiting for?"

The nurse did a double-take, followed by an eye rub. "I thought I saw… Never mind."

Although invisible, Jennie and Worthington moved out of the way of the nurses and let them do their thing. There was a small utility closet—a metal container with thin doors—which they climbed into and watched as the nurses brought out the defibrillator and worked on chest compressions.

Given that the poor girl had a lot of internal organ problems, Jennie had to give it to Diane. She didn't hold back.

Jennie supposed a life of pain was almost always going to be better than death. *Little did they know.*

They worked on the poor girl for fifteen minutes before a doctor arrived and officially pronounced her dead. The head nurse made a note on the clipboard and arranged it so that the gurney was removed from the ward, and for Carolyn to be taken down to the morgue.

Jennie and Worthington followed them through the hospital, standing directly beside the nurses in the elevator. At one point, it was so crowded that Jennie found herself standing *inside* someone and had to hold back a slight chuckle when the nurse who'd inadvertently occupied Jennie's space shivered and complained about the temperature.

The nurse's colleague shook his head. "It's just the morgue, Susan. Honestly, when will you get over it? People die. That's part of the job."

"It's not that, it's…" She couldn't explain what she was feeling.

The frigid room was illuminated by rows of fluorescent lighting. Along the far wall were the rows of metal lockers containing the bodies of those who had passed in the hospital and were awaiting either autopsy or exportation to their final resting places.

Jennie passed through the double doors leading into the autopsy room.

Worthington hesitated outside the door.

Jennie noticed his absence and poked her head through the door. "Are you coming in or not?"

"It's going to stink in there, isn't it?" Worthington complained.

Jennie rolled her eyes. "That's a common misconception. The majority of bodies in there have hardly had the chance to decompose. You might get the odd post-life fart, but otherwise, the smell is similar to the inside of an empty fridge."

Worthington gave Jennie a Look.

Jennie sighed and grabbed Worthington by the wrist. "Fine. The fridge you last smelled forty years ago when you were alive. Get over it and get your arse in here."

Worthington gulped and allowed himself to be pulled.

"We've got to stop meeting like this," a thin, gravelly voice crooned as the nurses put the brakes on the gurney and stepped away. A man who looked like an insect pretending to be a human handed his clipboard to the head nurse. He was tall and frail and hunched over with his hands rubbing his knuckles.

Diane gave him a stern look. "That gets funnier every time you say it, Durst. You might need a new line if you're ever planning on getting out of this human refrigerator."

Durst grinned, the expression painful to watch. "You can't beat the classics, though."

Diane shook her head. "You can't polish a turd, either, but I don't see that stopping you."

The nurses swept out the door as quickly as they could, leaving Durst behind to hover over the body.

"Poor girl," Durst croaked. He shook his head. "Taken in the prime of her life. Don't you worry, we've got a place for you right over here."

He half-galloped over to the lockers and pulled out a long metal tray. "Keaton, I need you."

Keaton, a man who was the polar opposite of Durst, appeared from a door at the back of the room. He was the same height, but he was at least three times as wide, and his arms were thick with muscle.

He glided over to the bed without a word and picked the body up. He placed her with surprising delicacy onto the tray poking out of the lockers like a robot's tongue and gently slid it closed.

Durst hesitated a moment, abandoning the sheets of the chart to talk to Keaton as he passed. "Pretty little thing, isn't she?" His tongue flicked over his lips obscenely.

Keaton half-turned on his way back to the office. "Don't do that, man. You know it gives me the creeps."

"Charming pair, aren't they?" Jennie whispered.

Durst's ears pricked up. "Did you hear that?"

"It's nothing. Just your imagination," Keaton called from the other room, where the flicker of a TV and the theme song to *Pretty Little Liars* was playing.

Durst busied himself at a nearby desk, resting his head in his hand as he digested the information on the new arrival.

Jennie was about to cross over and read the papers when Worthington grabbed her shoulder, a sudden panic on his face.

"What? What is it?" Jennie whispered as quietly as she could manage.

Worthington thumbed toward the door, while Durst's eyes scoured the room.

The coroner stuck a finger in his ear and gave it a wriggle.

Jennie could hear it now. Footsteps coming toward them. More than that, she could *feel* that something wasn't quite right. Over the years, she had learned to trust her instincts, and in this case, her instincts were telling her to hide.

But where?

Jennie grabbed Worthington and shoved him toward the lockers. His body disappeared behind the metal, and she vaguely heard his utterance of disgust. She looked around, saw a room divider behind Durst's desk, and flitted over, managing to hide just as a knock came at the door.

"Just a second," Durst called, irritation in his voice.

Jennie peeked above the divider and watched Durst cross the room.

When he opened the door, he couldn't see anyone standing there. He shrugged and closed the door, then returned to his desk, totally oblivious to the chuckling specter who had just stepped inside.

The specter checked Durst's clipboards, then made their way toward Carolyn's drawer.

CHAPTER NINE

The specter glided silently across the morgue without a care in the world. He wore a hospital nightgown that blew open behind him and showed Jennie things she'd rather not see, but there was confidence in his gait as he traced his finger in the air and looked for the correct number of the drawer.

"Ah!" he muttered.

He gripped the locker door, and a ghostly projection of the tray peeled away from the real thing, looking like a holographic replica had taken its place. On the tray was the pale, spectral body of Carolyn Hurst.

The specter leaned down until he was nose to nose with the girl. "Wakey, wakey," he shouted, his face hysterical. "Rise and shine!"

Jennie expected Durst to jump up in the air with a triumphant, "Aha! I knew it!" She was disappointed to find he sat with his eyes half-closed, leaning over the stack of paperwork in front of him.

She flushed, remembering that only certain specters could talk in a frequency that could be heard by humans.

There was a high-pitched scream and the spectral form of

Carolyn sat up suddenly as if waking from a nightmare. She looked around, her neck almost turning a full one-eighty, and screamed some more.

"Easy, easy," the male specter reassured Carolyn with a dark chuckle. "I know, I know. This is never the easiest bit to explain to a baby specter, particularly one as young as you. Here's the ten-second summary. You're dead. You died. You're no longer living. Your heart stopped beating. There's no more oxygen in your body. Life is over, and you now have a choice to make. How did I do? Did that cover it?"

Carolyn's face dropped. If she wasn't already as pale as a specter, she would've turned white. "I'm...I'm dead?"

The specter sighed. "Which variation of that sentence are you struggling with, dear? Do you want me to say it all again?"

Carolyn shook her head. "No. It's just, I was walking near the Plaza. Then..." She held a palm to her temple, trying to remember. "The car came out of nowhere. The next thing I knew, I was..."

"Dead!" the man snapped loud enough to make Carolyn jump.

I really don't like that guy, Jennie thought. *Toying with her is no way to introduce a new-born specter to the afterlife.*

The man looked at his watch, although the hands no longer moved. "I'm sorry to push this along, darling, but I've got places to be. Do you know how many people are dying here at the moment? Enough to fill a semi-truck, and then some. Every friggin' day!"

His words were cheery, a huge smile breaking his face. It was almost as though he was discussing the fact that it was going to be a beautiful day, and the Knicks had just won the NBA.

"So, here's the deal," he continued. "You're dead. I've covered that. But you have a choice to make. If you're happy to end your life and travel into the great beyond, then lay back, close your eyes and kiss goodbye to all your Earthly connections. You only get one shot at this, and it has to be quick."

He held up a finger. "If, on the other hand, you have unfinished business and wish to roam the world a little longer—which I'd highly advise, given that you likely just graduated from diapers to your big-girl panties and have yet to see the world—then I suggest sticking around as a specter." As he said the last word in his best spooky voice, he raised his arms.

"This is all so much to take in," Carolyn whimpered. "I can't be dead. I was in a car. Cody...he was there with me." Her eyes widened. "Is Cody okay?"

The specter shrugged. "Cody is..."

"My boyfriend!"

The specter paused for a second, cheeks puffed as if he was about to spew another round of irritating vitriol. Only this time, he showed the first ounce of compassion that Jennie had witnessed.

"Fine, hold on," he told her, as he stamped over to the desk and rifled through the papers. This time, the sheets really did fly through the air, exploding in great bursts and floating to the ground like large fallen leaves.

Durst's eyes grew wide as he gripped the table and leaned back in the chair, watching the papers fly by themselves. "Er, Keaton?"

"Not now! They're just about to announce Alison's killer. I've waited five seasons for this!"

"Yes. *Now*, Keaton!"

The specter finished his rifling, satisfied by what he'd seen. He crossed back over to Carolyn, just as Keaton appeared in the doorway.

He looked down at the papers littering the floor, eyes trailing several leaves still falling. He held a can of Dr. Pepper in one hand with a straw sticking out the top. "Something the matter, boss? Another one of your fits?"

"Another..." Durst choked on his words. "It wasn't me!"

"Are you sure?" Keaton asked, clearly unconvinced. "You

know what you're like when you fall asleep on the job. Night terrors and limb spasms. That's the fourth time this week."

Durst flung his bony hands up in frustration. "It wasn't... I didn't..."

Keaton raised the straw to his lips and slurped. He turned back to the office, muttering, "Can't believe I put the girls on pause for this. I've gotta find somewhere new to work. Surrounded by damn crazy people."

A moment later, the sound of the TV show resumed. Durst was left flummoxed by his desk, his mind clearly whirring as he tried to work out whether something had just happened, or if he'd imagined it all.

"Sorry about that," the specter mumbled, returning his attention to Carolyn. "No sign of a Cody on the dead sheets. Maybe he's still in ICU, but I can't confirm that. There's not enough time." He checked his watch again. "You've got approximately two minutes until the decision is made for you and you are sent off to the ether. Now, what's it going to be?"

Carolyn's lip wobbled. She muttered to herself.

From across the room, Jennie could make out the words "investment," "family," "love," and "wedding."

The specter tapped his watch. "Tick-tock, Carolyn. Time's running out."

"I choose life!" Carolyn blurted. "I'm only twenty-four, goddammit. I choose life."

"You mean, death," he corrected.

Carolyn frowned. "I mean life. Living in the after*life*."

"Yeah, but you can't undo death," he told her. "You're still dead."

"Really?" she asked. "You're making me make the biggest decision of my life, and you're arguing semantics?"

The specter fell silent, then added in a hushed voice, "Biggest decision of your *death*."

Carolyn threw her arms up and yelled in exasperation. "Just make the damn thing happen!"

"Big mouth for such a small girl," the specter remarked. "But you don't need me for that. It's already done."

"What do you mean it's done?" Carolyn demanded. "I don't feel any different."

The specter shrugged. "Well, technically, the choice isn't in your hands. Did you really think that' was how death worked? Truth is, some automatically go to the dark side, while others stick around as specters. Most of those who remain have unfinished business that even they may not be aware of, but many just cross over into the big beyond without a chance to argue."

"You just made me do all that…for fun?"

The specter grinned. "Partly. The other part is that you now know you would have chosen this life—"

"Aha! So it is *life*?—"

"I meant 'death,'" he told her.

Carolyn gave him a sharp look. "But you said 'life.'"

"*Anyway*," the specter continued, "here it is. Your afterlife. Your chance to watch over your loved ones and help them. The afterlife can be *super* difficult to navigate, so I'm here to make you an offer. Give you a chance to make your afterlife easier."

Carolyn was skeptical. "*You*? The guy who just tricked me into thinking I had a choice?"

"I know." The specter smirked. "Ironic, huh? This part of the job is lonely. I have to have my fun somehow."

Carolyn looked away. "You know, I've only just met you, and I hate you."

The specter stroked his chin. "Seems fair. However, this time, you really do have an option."

"And what's that?" she asked.

"In the afterlife, there are paths you can choose. Allegiances you can make that will benefit you and make it so you're never alone again. Mentors and guardians who can help you find your feet and become the best version of you in the afterlife. I can introduce you to them."

Carolyn debated this for a second, overwhelmed by the information she was receiving.

Jennie felt a little sorry for her, to have had her whole life whipped out from beneath her feet, and now she had to process and choose a way to navigate a world she hadn't even known existed.

It had been similar for her, in a way. Although Jennie was still human, the moment she had first uncovered her gift with specters had unleashed a whole new reality for her.

As a child, she had heard their voices wherever she went. Voices that her childish imagination told her were nothing more than friends who lived in her head. She would play with them, ask them questions when her parents were in the other room, invite them over for tea.

As she'd grown older, they'd started taking shape in front of her. She'd thought at the time that she had given them their voices, faces, and personalities, but she'd later worked out, after a late-night conversation with her parents in which she had spent most of the night telling them about a portly monk she'd met, that there was something more tangible to them than that.

For one thing, how could Jennie have invented monks in her head, when she had no idea what monks were?

It wasn't until they started performing for her and following her commands that she realized something was different for her.

When her parents held parties, she would harness her powers to get the ghosts to bring her objects behind the adults' backs. Soon enough, the other kids stayed away or bullied her. She grew reclusive and started to withdraw inside herself.

Why did she need *real* friends, when she could harness the friends around her and make them do her bidding?

The climax of it all came when Jennie turned eighteen.

She still remembered his name.

Major James Richer had been following her around for a while, obsessed by the girl who could talk to specters. He had befriended her and told her his story. He believed he would go down in the history books, not for the glory of some triumphant war effort, but for being the first man to have been killed by injuries sustained in a car crash.

"It wasn't so bad, I suppose," the major had been telling Jennie as he accompanied her down the street while she walked back home from an errand.

It was then that a group of teenage boys saw Jennie talking to herself. They knew her, of course. The whole street knew to look the other way when the girl "touched by spirits" walked by, but on that day, Jennie'd had enough.

Her anger was immediate. She'd latched onto the major and had him hurl himself at the boys. They didn't know what hit them, but they'd understood that floating in the air, held aloft by the back of their pants, was the result of their teasing.

That had been the final straw for Jennie, the alert flag that had drawn her parents toward finding a proper way to deal with her gift. When the Queen's Service had come to investigate what the spectral problems had been about, they had been grateful for a solution.

Jennie still recalled the words, eerily dissimilar to the ones the specter in the morgue was saying to Carolyn.

"Do you promise to honor and swear unfaltering fealty to the Spectral Plane?"

Spectral Plane? The specter's voice bought Jennie back to the present.

"To honor and protect the Spectral Plane within all reasonable boundaries of the existence of your death? To unite under the banner of the moon, and ensure liberty and freedom for America? Will you swear to forsake all others, including the Winter Court, the crown, and Her Paranormal Majesty?" The specter offered a hand.

Carolyn looked alarmed. She stared at it without comprehension.

"One more step, and you are free," the specter urged.

Jennie felt anger well up inside her. This girl didn't know the options. She didn't know the alternatives. Surely every new specter should at least be given all the facts? Be shown all the right information before making a choice?

Carolyn's hand moved slowly toward the specter's.

"*Thief!*" The voice came from the door. "Liar!"

The specter, Carolyn, and Jennie spun to see a man standing in front of the door. He wore a large white wig, his face was powdered, and he had a beauty spot on his cheek. He wore a jacket last fashionable in the Georgian era over a shirt with ruffles, and his dark shoes shone under the fluorescents.

The gowned specter turned with fury on his face. "You again?"

"Who else?" The new arrival spoke in an aristocratic British accent. "I am here on orders from the queen to ensure that new specters choose the correct allegiance when they swear their fealty. You cannot imagine that this young lady wishes to dilly-dally with your ridiculous rebellion when there is a power greater, more loving, and kinder to choose from?"

From inside the morgue's lockers, a muffled voice cried, "Charles? Is that you?"

The specter's eyebrows raised. He crossed to the lockers and opened a spectral projection of the drawer to reveal Worthington lying uncomfortably next to a dead body.

"Worthington?" Charles erupted in glee. "Worthington Conrad!"

Worthington hopped out of the drawer and patted himself down. He embraced Charles, then held him at arm's length. "I hoped I would run into you at some point on this excursion."

Charles clapped. "I'd heard you were traveling across the sea to assist on this side of the Pond. How the devil are you doing?"

"Oh, you know," Worthington told him amiably. "I can't complain."

Carolyn balled up her fists. The lights flickered as she erupted into a deafening shout. "Will someone tell me what the fuck is going on?"

The gowned specter opened his mouth to speak but was disrupted when Jennie appeared from behind the divider. "I'm sorry Carolyn, but you're being misled. You should know what your options are."

"Who's she?" Charles asked. He gave a slight tilt forward and sniffed. "She doesn't smell like a specter."

The gowned specter turned toward Carolyn suddenly and extended his hand again. "Quick, Carolyn. Before it's too late."

Carolyn tucked her hands beneath her arms. "Hold on; I want to hear what they have to say."

"There is a better road," Jennie explained, walking through Durst, who was looking at the flickering lights with a terrified expression. "There is a better power to align yourself with. The paranormal court, which is ruled by Queen Victoria. Swear your allegiance to the crown, and you will be under the wing of *the* oldest and most revered organization to exist in the afterlife."

"Then this Spectral Plane is just, what?" Carolyn asked.

"They're nobodies," Charles told her, his lip curling in disgust. "Imposters. Revolters. Those who have taken up a new fight against the crown and wish to see it torn down. They're not the first group, and they certainly won't be the last."

"Revolters?" Jennie thought. *The guy might have been able to speak the queen's English, but even she knew "revolters" wasn't a real word.*

"Oh, shut your filthy British yap, Lord Tight-ass." The gowned specter scowled. "We know your game. You've been recruiting evil fuckers left, right, and center and drafting them for your cause. Murderers, rapists, drug dealers, you don't give a shit who you filter into your precious *Court.*"

Charles placed a hand on his chest. "Excuse me?"

The specter pointed an accusatory finger at Charles. "You've gotten so concerned with bringing in the aristocracy and the pompous fuckers into your service that you've forgotten what counts. At one point, even I considered joining your cause, but what you've been doing lately is disgusting. We of the Spectral Plane can't stand it." He whirled once more to Carolyn. "Please, Carolyn. Would you rather spend eternity with the free, or under the thumb of a selfish tyrant who cares more about keeping the throne than the people she lives to serve?"

Carolyn debated her options. She looked at the gowned specter's hand and shook it. "I choose the free."

The gowned specter cheered. He snapped his fingers, and an explosion momentarily blinded the others. When it faded into nothing, they were in the dark. The lights in the morgue had all gone out, and there was no sound but the soft echo of a cackle.

"Well, I think that went well," Worthington muttered sarcastically.

Jennie sighed. "Shut up, Worthington."

CHAPTER TEN

The Plaza, New York City, Present Day

"Someone needs to tell me what in damnation is going on in this city," Jennie commanded.

Jennie had taken Charles back to her suite at the Plaza and immediately mixed herself a drink, combining ingredients from the minibar to make herself something that looked like cloudy lemonade, but was garnished with an umbrella and a spiral of orange peel.

Charles and Worthington looked absurd together-Worthington, the former Beefeater, and Charles, the pale-faced former revolutionary, both sitting upright in leather armchairs in a modern penthouse suite. Charles had one leg crossed over the other, while Worthington adjusted the straps of his far-too-big hat.

"You saw it yourself," Charles answered. "The Spectral Plane is a nuisance who appeared several months ago and began plotting a rebellion against the crown. They've been lying to new specters by the dozen, beating any recruitment attempts we've made by offering a life better than the one we have to offer."

"What's better than service to the queen?" Worthington

replied. "She's the longest-reigning monarch of the paranormal court, her power so great that service can only reap bountiful rewards. What could be greater than that?"

"Freedom," Jennie answered quietly, though clearly not quite enough.

"What good is freedom in the afterlife?" Worthington snapped. "Freedom is dangerous. Freedom is anarchy. Do you think the world was built on a system of freedom? No. It was built underneath a hierarchy revolving around the powerful and the forgiving."

Charles nodded. "You saw what happened with the American Revolution, didn't you? Thousands of soldiers dead, just for the sake of freedom. Will freedom bring our lives back? No. Freedom just sent humans by the thousands into the great abyss. If America had learned at the time that the crown's rule is compassion and love, none of that would have happened."

"I thought it was a good thing that America got its freedom?" Jennie retorted, instantly throwing her hands up in a defensive gesture as Charles glared at her. "Don't the Americans love their freedom? And, no. Do you really think I look old enough to *remember* the Revolution?"

"But look what it did to colonial rule," Charles replied, ignoring Jennie's last comment. "The moment Britain lost America, its Empire began to collapse."

"So?" Jennie commented. "For humans, independence was the way forward."

"You are thinking too much with your 'living brain,'" Charles reprimanded. "Think of it this way. The paranormal world has centered around the British monarchy for thousands of years. Every time a reigning monarch dies, they take over the mantle of the paranormal king or queen."

"There are no other superpowers," Worthington replied. "A few small rebel groups, but none with the strength of the crown. That's how the paranormal world keeps on turning. Without order and loyalty, what is there left to keep everything under control? You're a human who understands specters, right? You know what happens when specters turn down a bad path. It's chaotic. It's worse than anarchy. It's *dangerous* for humans."

"Fine, fine. I hear you," Jennie relented. She took a long sip of her drink and looked out over Central Park. The trees were dark, the outline of the park illuminated by the sodium arcs.

"There's just one thing that makes no sense to me, though," she told Charles. "That guy back there, he said that the caliber of converted was lessening? That the queen was allowing scum and dirtbags to serve the crown? What did he mean by that?"

"Oh, you know how it is." Charles chuckled dismissively. "Enemy propaganda at its finest. They're hardly going to tell the people they're converting to their cult that everything is sunshine and rainbows on the other side, are they? No. I wouldn't pay attention to them. In fact, it's been my job to try to help them see the opposite."

"And what a fine job you're doing," Worthington told him dryly.

"I beg your pardon?" Charles sat up straight in his chair and pointed his finger at Worthington. "You haven't been here, Conrad. America is different from England. Did you know that Americans believe their trousers are pants? Have you ever heard anything so preposterous?"

Jennie and Worthington both shook their heads.

"Whatever is going on," Jennie told them. "We need to find the truth behind it all. I had begun to think that the Spectral Plane was nothing more than a human organization who believed in ghosts but couldn't prove it. Now we've discovered there's a whole group of specters with the same name out there."

"Maybe they were accidental conversions?" Worthington suggested.

Jennie sat on the countertop and served another measure of the cocktail into her glass. "What do you mean?"

Worthington scratched his head. "Well, when a spirit swears to someone in the afterlife, the words have to bind them to *someone*, right? We swear to the crown, and Victoria earns our allegiance. If the Spectral Plane members *were* humans, forcing people to swear to…whoever, then the specters must have found *someone* to bind to."

"What do you mean, if the Spectral Plane members were humans?" Charles said. "I've been dealing with their kind for months."

"Exactly," Worthington continued. "So, there must be a *leader* to whom they bind themselves to. Someone they serve above all others and take their commands from. Find the leader, and we find the solution to breaking them apart and returning the status quo."

"Sounds like a plan." Jennie drained her drink and hopped off the counter. "Come. There are still a few hours before dawn."

Baxter followed the two Spectral Plane specters through the narrow alleys and down a set of stairs leading to the subway. The tunnels were quiet, the lights casting an eerie gloom over the tiled walls. Occasionally he could hear the distant rumble of the trains.

There were very few people around at this hour. Those who were seemed to either not speak English or had made their home outside the tunnels. All were eager to avoid the possibility of rain while praying they wouldn't get shifted by Security or the cops. A man with a grizzled beard was sitting under a tattered blanket playing the harmonica, his dusty hat filled with nothing more than a few measly dimes.

The pair took a left, heading down a long tunnel that curved to the right. When they reached its end, they walked out onto a train platform and jumped down onto the tracks.

Baxter followed, using a hand to balance himself on the drop. When he stood, he saw the others had gotten some distance on him.

He picked up his pace, only vaguely aware of the train approaching from behind. The brakes screeched as the train pulled to a stop, leaving Baxter's head sticking out of the floor of the farthest carriage. Just a few feet away from him, a man was sitting with a broadsheet open, his eyes occasionally flicking to a woman who wore hardly anything.

She chewed gum and fluttered her eyelashes, clearly on the hunt for possible business from the man.

Baxter snorted a laugh, and soon enough, the train pulled away from him. When it disappeared down the tunnel, he saw the other two specters take a right and followed them.

Where better for a secret organization to hide than down in the tunnels where the rats play?

They finally reached a doorway which read DANGER, TUNNEL UNSTABLE.

The pair opened the door and paused, waiting patiently for Baxter, who froze on the spot.

"You saw me?" Baxter asked.

"Let's just say you're hardly the type to remain unnoticed," Baseball Cap told him. "A seven-foot-tall guy trying to sneak through a tunnel? Come on, man, get your ass up here."

He ushered Baxter inside, where darkness was waiting for him.

"Either of you two bring a light? I stopped smoking years ago," Baxter quipped.

The other two looked at each other. Their faint spectral glow was enough to see each other by, but not enough to light the tunnel.

"You're a funny man," the specter wearing a baseball cap and a thick sweater replied. "The boss will like that. We need funny on our side of the tracks."

Baxter laughed. "I get it. Tracks, because we're in the subway?"

"Don't give him the satisfaction," the second specter, a woman with a gaunt, skeletal face and thin wisps of hair, croaked. "He already thinks *he's* Mister Funny Man."

Baseball Cap frowned. "Just because you lost your funny bone in 'Nam."

The woman shook her head, her face straight. "Correction, I lost my funny bone in World War I. You think malnourishment like this comes from living in an era where food wasn't rationed? Damn shame that you live as a specter how you died in your life."

"Preach," Baxter agreed.

"What's wrong with you?" she asked.

"Oh, I died in an explosion," Baxter answered. "Blown sky-high while tinkering with an automobile."

"You look all right to me," Baseball Cap told him.

"I suppose I was lucky," Baxter replied. "My heart was the first to go. The shock of it killed me before the burns did. Though…" He tugged down his collar to reveal an inch-long slash on his neck with a piece of metal sticking out of it. "This bastard found its way in before my heart gave out. Now I've got to live forever with shrapnel in my throat."

"I feel so sorry for you," the woman told him flatly, her cheeks so sunken that it looked like she was sucking them in.

They followed the tunnel, taking the journey slower than the rest of it. Soon enough, Baxter heard the muttering of voices. There was some laughter, some cheering and, impossibly, music coming from up ahead.

"The Spectral Plane is a jovial bunch," Baseball Cap told him. "To think, I nearly threw it all away and pledged allegiance to the crown." He spat on the floor. "Couldn't imagine a worse fate."

Baxter felt the first tingle of nerves. He had drawn out the information from Joan and found out all about the Spectral

Plane. Had heard her stories of their mission, and the revolution they were building toward.

After a considerable time talking to the woman's mushed lips, Baxter had decided that he'd go and visit the Planes and discover first-hand what they had to offer. As far as he was aware, only Joan and her men knew of his brief rendezvous with the human woman and the Beefeater, and so maybe there was a chance he could join the cause. Finally pick a side.

Or at least discover first-hand what was on offer before choosing which party to side with. After all, if things carried on the way they were going, soon enough, there would be war.

The tunnel opened up into a large underground cavern—what might once have been a subway station used back in the early days of the foundation of the rail networks. Now, faded ad posters hung crookedly on the walls, their text faded and the pictures all but gone. Sitting along the platform edge were dozens of specters, each wearing a spectral pendant that held the symbol of Mjölnir, a runic working of Thor's hammer.

"Why Mjölnir?" Baxter whispered to the others.

The man smiled at Baxter. "Because the Spectral Plane is gonna break the shackles of oppression. For that, we need the power of the mighty gods. The weapon of the breaker of chains, the God of Thunder." He raised his voice suddenly. "We are the breakers of shackles!"

All heads present turned to the chamber entrance as every specter raised a fist and cried, "Awoo! Awoo!"

Baxter felt his nervousness return. *Have I accidentally entered a cult?*

Several specters were in huddles, deep in conversation. A few were asleep on the floor.

"Got a hell of a group down here, huh?" Baxter whispered.

"It's the only safe space we could find," Baseball Cap replied. "The forgotten parts of the city where people wouldn't even think to look."

"It's like you've got something to hide."

The woman smirked. "For now."

Baxter hopped onto the platform after them and was guided toward an abandoned train. Its wheels were rusted to the tracks, and the windows were smashed and covered in a fine layer of grime and dirt.

"Hey, boss! We've got a new recruit!"

Some of the tension in Baxter's shoulders eased when he saw the man in the pristine suit emerge from the next carriage. He had a white rose on his lapel and a hole in his stomach. "I wondered when we'd be seeing you."

"Tobias?" Baxter laughed, making to run over to his friend and shake his hand until he felt two sets of arms holding him back. He turned to either side and saw Baseball Cap and Skeletor gripping him firmly. "What's going on?"

Tobias laced his fingers behind his back. "Times are changing, dear friend. The spectral world is due to have a catastrophic shift, and soon enough, every specter will have to pick a side. You've done well choosing the Spectral Plane."

The cogs in Baxter's mind whirred. He didn't like the expression on Tobias' face. "I thought you were a neutral?"

"I was, at one point in my life." He chuckled. "The truth is that no one can be neutral forever. *He's* made that very clear. I've found that the best way to nudge recruits in the right direction is to go undercover in the places where the neutrals gather. You can see my logic, right?"

"I suppose." Baxter wriggled against those holding him firm but couldn't work free. "How about you tell your hounds to release me so we can talk as free men?"

Tobias took a seat on one of the carriage chairs and crossed one leg. "Didn't you hear me, Baxter? No man or woman will be free for long. Sooner or later, we all have to decide. The *real* question is, where does your allegiance lie? Is it with your brothers within the Spectral Plane, or with those *scum* you brought with you to the party?"

Baxter's eyes widened. "*You* set those goons on them?"

"A carefully placed whisper can travel far in the right conditions." Tobias grinned. "Representatives of the Winter Court are *not* welcome within *our* city."

"Your city?" Baxter's eyebrows raised.

"Actually," Tobias stood up at the sound of footsteps and motioned with an arm toward another figure walking through the carriage doors. "It'll soon be *his* city."

Baxter's face darkened as the figure approached. He fought against the pair holding him but could not move.

Oh, Bax. I think you've made a grave error in judgment...

Brooklyn, New York, Present Day

Worthington's nose wrinkled as he looked down at the bags of trash piled around his feet in the dumpster. "So, this is your idea of spy work?"

Jennie clutched the edge of the dumpster and stared through the small slit in the lid, observing the wooden door of the old redbrick building. The graffiti was actually rather impressive. Not the kind created by prepubescent children with bad attitudes, but by urban artists looking for a decent canvas to spray. "Sometimes you've got to stand in filth to capture filth."

Worthington scoffed. "You're just full of whimsy, aren't you?"

Jennie ignored his sarcasm. "I'm glad you catch on quick. Shame Charles couldn't join us for this part."

"You hardly gave him the option when you told him to, and I quote, 'Leave us the fuck alone to do our task for the queen, while you fuck off and do whatever the fuck she told you to do.'"

Jennie chuckled. "I'm eloquent, aren't I?"

"That's one word for it," Worthington replied.

The street was empty, as it had been several nights ago. In the hour or so they'd been waiting, they'd seen several specters pass through the door and down into the place where mortals now used the old catacombs to mature cheeses. A few had since re-emerged and floated down the street, but none of the type she was looking for.

"Even if they *are* with the Spectral Plane, do you think they're going to wear it on their sleeves?" Worthington asked. "You're never going to be able to identify them from afar."

"Oh, I think we'll have a sneaking suspicion," Jennie replied. "Those goons who attacked us the other night were of a certain sort, wouldn't you say? I could have predicted they'd be batting for the enemy."

"But you didn't," Worthington noted.

"But I could've," Jennie shot back.

"But you didn't." Worthington squirmed, raising his feet up above the bags.

"Will you please stand still?" Jennie complained. "You're distracting me."

Worthington glared at Jennie. "Oh, I'm sorry. Is it inconvenient for you that I don't enjoy standing in other people's waste?"

Jennie gave him a sharp look. "Yes. Yes, it is."

Worthington huffed and stomped his feet. "What did I ever do to deserve getting stuck with you?" he muttered.

"The feeling's mutual," Jennie replied. "You know that my other specters actually appreciated being paired with me? They respected my work. Actually *helped* me to achieve my missions. They didn't spend every waking hour complaining and moaning."

"That's not what I heard," Worthington huffed. "Besides, I'm starting to think Her Majesty was testing me. If I can survive a mission across the Atlantic with you, I'll most definitely work my way into her A-Team. All I've got to do is keep you out of trouble, and make sure the job gets done."

Jennie snorted. "Yeah, well, good luck with that."

"What's that supposed to mean?" he demanded.

Jennie smirked. "Let's just say that there's a reason I've earned the moniker 'Rogue.'"

"Because you don't think before you act?" he asked.

Jennie considered her reply. "More like I get the job done by any means necessary. Sometimes the straight and narrow path isn't the best one to take. Sometimes you've got to blast holes in the wall to find a way through."

"How poetic."

"Well, I did once drop in on a meeting in The Eagle and Child with the Inklings. Got a few tips from the pros."

Worthington raised an eyebrow.

"You've never heard of them? Okay, how about J.R.R. Tolkien, C.S. Lewis, Charles Williams, and Hugo Dyson?"

"I'm familiar with the first two," Worthington admitted. "Not the others. Didn't Hugo invent the hoover?"

Jennie chuckled. "You really should brush up on your history. Hugo and the others used to meet every now and then to discuss their writing and works. Dyson and Williams were lesser-known. Actually, Dyson was pretty vocal *against* Tolkien's *The Lord of the Rings*, to the point where Tolkien ditched him and carried on with his writing anyway. If Dyson had had his way, Tolkien's estate and Peter Jackson would be out a fair few million."

Worthington gave her a skeptical look. "You can't possibly expect me to believe you sat down and shared a pint with two of the greatest fantasy writers of all time?"

Jennie shrugged. "Believe what you want. You should know that in an outfit like this…" She pointed to the cleavage straining at her corset, "a woman can eavesdrop on *any* conversation."

She returned her attention to the doorway just as a group of three specters emerged. They laughed loudly into the night, making no effort to keep themselves quiet.

"Just wait until the others hear about this," a woman with a shorn head and tattoos decorating her neck barked as they turned down the street. "Two recruits in one night. The boss is gonna be *very* happy."

Jennie waited until they were out of sight before raising the dumpster lid and leaping out of the trash. She rubbed small bits of debris from her leg, reached into a small pocket on her hip, and withdraw a vial of purple liquid.

She sprayed several blasts of the perfume over her legs, taking an extra few seconds to cover her body. She took a deep sniff. "Ah, just like roses."

"Shame perfume doesn't work on specters," Worthington complained.

Jennie rolled her eyes. "Right. Neither does trash. Now get your arse in gear. We've got specters to follow."

CHAPTER ELEVEN

Abandoned Subway, New York City, Present Day

Jennie frowned. "So, I think we lost them."

As the morning sun began to color the sky, Jennie and Worthington had followed the trio through the city. They remained a block behind and were easily able to catch up to see which way the trio was going. Considering there was hardly anyone around at that time, identifying them wasn't difficult.

They followed the specters over the Brooklyn Bridge and down into the subway station.

Jennie found herself feeling eerily at home, having spent a goodly amount of time on the London Underground back in England. The big cities had it figured out. Underground travel was *so* much faster than cars and taxis.

Apart from when the railways broke down.

On the walls were a series of posters in Perspex frames, advertising everything from Broadway shows to the latest fads in the wellness industry. The fluorescents occasionally flickered, causing Jennie to wonder whether it was because of the aged bulbs, or because of sudden waves of spectral activity.

Surely, if it was the latter, I would have felt it?

Then things got trickier. As they passed farther into the subway tunnels, they had less room to hide. Soon enough, it was a game of cat and mouse in which the only indication that they were on the right track was the ever-fading sound of the trio's voices as they laughed and discussed what they'd discovered at the spectral party.

One of them laughed. "You know she really thinks freedom is going to be an option, right? She was talking as though she had *years* before anything was going to happen."

"We'll see," the second added.

The first scoffed. "Just wait, soon the boss will have enough on his side to lead the rebellion. It's going to be like 1755 all over again."

"1775, idiot," the third corrected.

"What was 1755, then?"

"How about twenty years before the American Revolution?"

"Wow," Jennie muttered to Worthington as she leaned around a corner and watching them fade from view. "He's even worse with his history than you."

Worthington scowled but remained silent.

Several turnings later, they were well and truly lost. They reached a platform where a train had just pulled in and approached the carriage.

Jennie hesitated outside of the doors. "Can you see them anywhere?"

Worthington shook his head. "Beats me."

"I wish I could."

"Charming," Worthington replied.

When the train pulled away, they were left with nothing more than an empty track.

"They couldn't have just disappeared," Jennie muttered.

Worthington looked down his nose.

"Oh, you know what I mean." She hopped down onto the

tracks and looked up and down the tunnel. "You think they went along the tracks?"

"Or through the walls, or through the ceiling, or through the floor," Worthington replied. "Really, they could have gone anywhere."

Jennie shook her head. "I can *feel* them still." She took a few steps one way, then the other, finally finding a resolution. "The feeling is stronger this way. Come on."

Worthington glanced around nervously. "What about the trains?"

Jennie chuckled, already lost in the tunnel's darkness. "Don't worry. I've got it covered."

Alec McGuffin had worked through the night.

It was nearing morning, and there were only twenty minutes until his shift was over. A couple more stops, and he'd be home in time to be with his wife and son as they ate breakfast and wished him a good day.

Not that he'd see much of the day. Later that night, he'd be back in the subway system for another evening of ferrying the drunks and questionables around the city and calling the cops to break up fights when they happened.

Man, what has my life become?

The only positive thing Alec had in his life as a train driver was an unblemished record of never having to report a Diver.

"Diver" was the code name for those who jumped onto the tracks and got squished under the trains. Oftentimes, they were suicidal businesspeople with nothing to live for. Sometimes they were drunkards with a bad sense of balance. On occasion, there were teens who thought they could beat the trains and discover secrets in the tunnels.

Idiots. At least the kids don't frequent the trains at night. Lucky for me they're all home in bed.

Which was exactly where Alec planned to be heading in seventeen minutes.

He pulled the lever, set off the announcements for the next station, and felt the train build momentum as it began to speed down the track. The tunnel swallowed it. The only light came from the emergency lights, which looked like shooting stars as the train streaked past.

Alec kicked back, checked his watch—and something caught his eye.

A woman on the tracks. Instinctively, he reached for the emergency brake and yelped as the train lurched to a grinding stop. It happened in a moment. The train's momentum carried it forward another couple hundred feet or so before he found it came to a screeching halt.

Alec jumped out of the train and stood in front of it his hands on his hips, looking for any sign of the woman who he was certain had been there moments before.

But there was nothing. No blood, not a single hair flying through the air. Nothing. He jogged to the back of the train and looked down the tunnel. He called out, half-expecting a response, but nothing came.

Alec scratched his head, then pawed his eyes, wondering if perhaps he was getting too old for this shit. If his overtiredness was finally causing delusions.

I saw her! I saw her right there!

But had he?

Alec climbed back onto the train, gave a quick announcement to the passengers, and put the train back in motion. He made a mental note to update his supervisor on the situation, ready to apologize for causing the train to be delayed by several minutes.

At least my hundred-percent record is intact, he thought as the tunnel once more swallowed the train.

Jennie stood for a moment on the track, watching the train pull away.

"At least everyone's fine," she told Worthington, cutting off her connection to him.

Worthington breathed a sigh of relief. "Except for the train driver, who likely thinks he's gone crazy."

"Yeah, apart from him." Jennie nodded at a door etched into the tunnel's wall.

"Still, at least we stopped in the right place."

"How do you know that's where they went?" Worthington argued.

Jennie rolled her eyes. "For someone who's been dead for nearly fifty years, you'd think you'd have developed a better awareness for where the dead are lurking."

"Unfortunately, we weren't all blessed to have inherited your powers."

Jennie winked at him. "That's true."

They went through the door and walked toward the murmuring of voices they heard in the near distance. Jennie could feel something familiar. A specter who she'd come across before, only the trail was too faint to be able to pinpoint who it was she sensed.

Jennie closed her eyes and allowed her body to feel the spectral energies around her. "They've been recruiting the neutrals."

Worthington frowned. "How do you know?"

"Because some of them are here." Jennie said no more, just zeroed in on her powers and focused her attention on what was to come. No matter what happened, she needed to find out what was going on here. Her task was to put a stop to the new recruitment efforts and ensure that Queen Victoria's rule was obeyed.

Charles and Worthington were right. If spectral activity

wasn't governed by one unifying body, that would put mortals in a whole host of dangers.

The closer they got, the quieter the voices became. Jennie had a distinct feeling that they were being watched. Nonetheless, she continued on.

Worthington trailed a few feet behind with his guard up. He turned his head all the way around on his neck, looking for the enemy he expected to appear from the darkness at any moment.

Jennie found the spinning head trick amusing, of course. She was used to the way specters could play with their density and use their ethereal energy to do the seemingly impossible. Jennie had become more than familiar with the powers particular specters employed over the years. She had experimented with many herself, utilizing the energies of her companions for the benefit of them both whenever a dangerous situation presented itself.

Jennie had been in Slovenia back in 1941, tracking down a pedophile ring who had made a hidden section of the Postojnan caves their home. While on her journey, her handmade torch had been extinguished thanks to the dripping water from the rocks, and the sodden materials were too damp to rekindle.

She had sensed the specters in the cave the moment she had arrived, and in talking to them, she had discovered that a cave-in had killed a group of explorers several hundred years before.

It was one of these explorers who she'd been able to tap into and cast a light on the pitch-dark caves to finally bust the ring and rescue the four dozen children who had been kidnapped and imprisoned in the caves.

The criminals hadn't been able to work out why an orb of light was following Jennie around.

Jennie felt the specters around her in the here and now, but she continued walking as though there was nothing to fear. Her stride was confident, her head held high. She spied another door at the end of the corridor and reached for the handle.

A voice spoke from behind her. "Are you sure you want to do that?"

Jennie didn't bother turning around, just held the handle in her hand. "I've never been more certain of anything in my life."

The tunnel was suddenly illuminated by a blinding light, and dozens of hands grabbed Jennie and wrestled her to the floor.

CHAPTER TWELVE

London, England, 1887

Jennie beamed as the Savoy Hotel came into sight.

The Savoy was a marvel to behold, one of the hotels most often frequented by celebrities and politicians alike. Jennie had never seen anything like it. The foyer was a swath of marble, the guests wore evening gowns and suits, and the receptionist and valets said their "pleases" and "thank yous" as though the guests were royalty.

Samuel, Penelope, and Genevieve King most definitely weren't.

They had not been born among the aristocracy, but Jennie's father had skills that had propelled his family to the building situated directly beside the brand-new hotel.

Jennie practically leaped through the doors to the Savoy Theater, which had largely funded the erection of the Savoy Hotel. She ran along the lush red carpet that led hundreds of nightly patrons into a whole host of shows and theatrical delights.

Her eyes filled with wonder at the electric lightbulbs illuminating the walkway, a glow of pride inside that it was her father who had led the team that delivered the gift of electricity to the world's finest city.

Jennie's father lifted her onto his arms at the back of the theater. The seats sloped down in long rows toward one of the largest stages Jennie had ever seen.

"See all this?" Jennie's mother asked. "Your father helped make all this happen. Everything you have now is a product of your father and his team."

Samuel took a deep breath. "Can you smell that? That's history in the making, and you're a big part of that."

Jennie smiled, her eyes filled with wonder. It had been a while since her father had let her visit the site of his work, but now that she was old enough to wander around unsupervised, he finally allowed her the privilege.

Samuel kissed Jennie's head and let her down to explore. "Just don't go too far." He grinned, snuggling an arm around his Penelope.

Jennie explored every inch of that building in the weeks that followed. She familiarized herself with the bar, the dressing rooms, the trap beneath the stage. There were rooms for utilities, some for directive creation, and one at the back to test and play with the sound.

There were actors and dancers, directors, and composers. Each person Jennie met treated her as though she were a part of the family, inviting her in for talks and letting her play their instruments. Soon enough, she had become a part of the furniture of the place.

And the voices. There were so many voices here.

It was several days before the grand opening of the latest Gilbert & Sullivan extravaganza when Jennie first saw her—another little girl walking past the open door to the dressing room.

Jennie was sitting in the dressing room chair at the time, brushing her hair and staring at herself in the mirror. She was a thin girl, her face paler than most other kids. She blinked twice when the girl went past.

"Hello?" Jennie called, sure she hadn't seen any other girls visiting when her father had gotten to work this morning. Several of the main stage lights had blown, and he was busy working on a solution to stop the bulbs from popping when left on for too long.

Jennie hopped off the chair and turned down the corridor. She saw the girl disappear around the corner and decided to follow.

Only, when Jennie rounded the corner, the girl was gone. She kept an eye out for her all day. She even went as far as to ask her mother but was told that there was no one else in the building with them that day. The performers had all taken a final day off before their eight-week run began.

There was definitely no one there who matched the girl's description.

Jennie felt herself grow ashamed. She had spoken to her mother before about voices she had heard, and people she thought she saw, and it hadn't been met with the greatest of responses.

But this girl was different, Jennie was certain. She had *seen* her with her own eyes.

On the day of the first show, the seats were filled. There was not a single space left in the theater. Newspaper reporters came from around the country to write reviews and opinion pieces on the show.

Jennie was sitting in the wings entranced by the incredible voices of the opera singers when she saw the girl appear in the doorway to her left. She turned to her mother, not sure whether to tell her what she was seeing, and instead settled on asking to visit the bathroom.

Her mother, glassy-eyed and enthralled by the performance, nodded and told her to return quickly.

Jennie found the girl in the corridor staring up at a poster and reading the words. "Are you quite well?"

The little girl was no more than six years of age. She turned her head, confusion on her face. "Excuse me?"

"I asked if you needed any help," Jennie repeated cheerfully.

The girl looked down the corridor as if she believed Jennie had been speaking to someone else. "What year is it?"

"1887, silly." Jennie chuckled. "Are you lost? Do you need help finding your mummy?"

The little girl's eyes widened. She suddenly turned and ran down the corridor.

"Wait! Come back!" Jennie called after her.

Being taller and a little older, Jennie gained on the girl. The girl navigated down corridors and through doorways as if she knew all the secrets the theater had to offer. What she didn't account for was that Jennie was just as familiar with the back corridors and where the doorways led, so she couldn't shake her off.

It was only when the little girl reached a dead end that Jennie stopped and put her hands on her knees, gasping for breath. "Please, speak to me. Who are you?"

The girl paused long enough to look over her shoulder. She shook her head, disbelief in her eyes, and began to pass through the wall. Her body slipped through as if there was nothing there to block her.

Jennie's eyes widened. She was sweating, clumps of hair stuck to her forehead. The girl was a ghost!

"Stop." She said it so quietly that it was no wonder the girl didn't hear. "*Stop!*"

Her cry was so loud that several members of the audience looked for its source. Several of the singers paused for the briefest of moments but regained their composure and continued as if nothing had happened. Every light in the auditorium flicked at the speed of a hummingbird's wing.

The girl stopped, too.

Jennie watched with fascination as a small thread of shining energy appeared from her body and crawled toward the girl like some kind of ghostly worm. It stretched and stretched and stretched until it reached the girl, then connected to her like a thread-thin umbilical cord.

The girl looked shocked. "What are you doing?"

Jennie didn't answer. Instead, she obeyed her instinct and reached out. She pulled the girl back through the wall while remaining several meters away. She could feel a part of her controlling the ghost, a part of her connecting and becoming one in a way she had never felt before.

The girl fought for a few seconds, and then her fearful expression turned into a mask of fascination. She allowed herself to be pulled toward Jennie until she was only a foot or so away. "What *are* you?" she asked.

Jennie looked at her hands as if they were someone else's. "I don't know." She dropped to her knees, better to match the girl's height. "Did it hurt? Did I hurt you?"

The girl shook her head. She seemed to be in perfect health.

Aside from the fact she was dead, of course.

"You controlled me," she told Jennie.

"I'm sorry," Jennie blurted, finding her voice at last. "I just wanted to know who you are. I've been wanting to speak to someone like you forever, and I didn't want you to leave."

The little girl took her hand and smiled. "I was told we couldn't speak to your kind. That the connection was lost the moment I died."

"You're..." Jennie realized the thought of a few moments ago was fact. A weight she hadn't known she was carrying fell away from her.

"A ghost, yes," the girl replied with a giggle.

Jennie jumped up and down. "I knew it! I *knew* I wasn't mad! Mother and Father didn't believe I could hear ghosts, but I knew they were real. I knew all along. Tell me, what's your name? How did you die?"

Voices came down the corridor. Stewards called to investigate the disturbance during the performance. The little girl grabbed Jennie's hand and pulled her through the wall, taking her into a dark, quiet room. They waited until the footsteps receded and the stewards left, scratching their heads.

When things fell quiet, the girl told Jennie her story. "My name is Annabelle Lyons. I was visiting the old Savoy building when a great fire ate it from the inside out. My parents managed to survive, but my lungs were overcome by the smoke."

Jennie's eyes widened. "How ghastly!"

"It was horrible," Annabelle recalled. "Even now, when I close my eyes, all I see is darkness."

"Same here," Jennie replied, closing her eyes and giggling.

Annabelle laughed. "What about you? What was that power you used back there?"

"I don't know," Jennie told her honestly. "That's never happened before. I've always been able to see and hear people like you, but I was never sure they could hear me. I didn't even know I could do…whatever that was."

"Try it again," the girl told her. She jumped to her feet and spread her arms wide.

Jennie was shocked. "What?"

Annabelle waved for Jennie to get up. "I'll stand over here, and you pull me toward you."

Jennie smiled. "If you're sure it didn't hurt."

They stood across the room from each other. "Are you ready?"

Annabelle nodded. "I'm ready!"

Jennie closed her eyes tried to recapture how she'd felt when she'd grasped Annabelle's energy. She concentrated and felt something strange inside of her, as though something was alive and wanted to get out. She grasped mentally, doing her best to catch it. But it was like trying to pluck a fish from a murky pond. The minute she thought she'd done it, the feeling slipped away.

"Anything?" Annabelle asked.

"Give me a moment." Jennie screwed her eyes shut, her face turning red.

She could feel it, somewhere inside. Knew it was there. She focused her attention on the slippery feeling, aiming to grasp it with both hands until finally, she had it. "Oh!"

The thread appeared again, crawling through the air from her midsection. This time it was slower, as though it were crawling in slow motion.

Annabelle's face was bright with excitement as the thread reached half the halfway point of the room. "Keep going! Almost there."

Jennie opened her eyes and saw the thread, and she felt an overwhelming surge of emotion. The energy connected with Annabelle, and now she could *feel* her ghostly friend. Feel her emotions, her power, her energy.

Annabelle chuckled loudly, the sound as if she were laughing from far off in a distant cave. "You did it!"

Jennie beamed. "I did it!" Her smile slipped as she felt something new and strange. Something *wrong*.

Annabelle's smile slipped. "Jennie? Jennie? What is it?"

Jennie couldn't answer. Her mouth flapped open and shut. She let out a sudden scream and collapsed to the floor, all her energy expended on building her connection to Annabelle.

It wouldn't be until after the performance that the stewards and cast members sent to hunt for Jennie stumbled across her unconscious body.

It would be several more years before Jennie learned to control her powers.

CHAPTER THIRTEEN

Abandoned Subway, New York City, Present Day

The voices were everywhere. All types of accents and dialects from many different time periods. Words Jennie hadn't heard spoken in decades, and some she had never heard spoken.

But she couldn't *see* any of it. All Jennie was aware of was the hands carrying her somewhere she couldn't see. The sack had been pulled over her head almost immediately, and now the specters were doing the work for her and saving her the energy of having to walk the final few miles to the finish line.

Always a good idea to save my energy.

Worthington was somewhere nearby. Occasionally, she heard snippets of his beautiful British blustering.

"Unhand me, you scoundrels!"

"Release me at once!"

"This is ridiculous! Don't you know who I am, you rotten cads?"

Meanwhile, Jennie remained silent. During the 1980s, she had taken a few months to go on a journey of self-discovery. After meeting a man in a London bar who specialized in teaching yoga and meditation practices, she had taken his advice and taken the next flight out of the UK.

Her journey had taken her to Budapest and then on to India. She spent time with the monks, and she was mentored by the yogis. During a four-week stint in Chattarpur, she had studied with a yoga instructor who had taught her the tenets of mastering self-control and how to regulate her heartbeat.

These lessons had provided invaluable knowledge and had gone a long way toward aiding in the work she had performed for the queen over the last hundred and forty years.

Particularly now, when she'd been bagged and was being carried by an unknown number of spectral assailants deep into the underground tunnels of New York City.

Jennie calmed herself, taking her mind back to her happy place. A time when she had first learned to control her powers. When her parents were alive, and life was simpler.

Finally, she felt herself being placed on the floor, and she heard Worthington shuffling frantically somewhere nearby. "At last. Now, remove this damn sack."

No answer.

They'd been left alone in silence.

Jennie looked inward, using her gift to feel around the room. The specters were still nearby, although Jennie couldn't get a precise count.

"Remove the bags."

A familiar voice.

Jesus. I've only been in the city for a few days, and already I've met everyone there is to meet.

The bags were whipped roughly off their heads, and the candlelight stung their eyes.

Jennie blinked, and the blurry face of someone she thought she'd meet along her path came into focus. "Lupe?"

Lupe looked surprised. "You know my name?" A grin appeared on his face. "I knew word of my work would spread."

Jennie wrinkled her nose in distaste. "Or maybe you just can't control your voice? You forgot that we were watching you in the park. You're not the most observant member of the Spectral Plane, are you?"

Lupe sat back smugly in his chair. For some reason, they had procured an old leather armchair and placed it in the center of the abandoned train carriage. Specters lined the fold-down seats while Jennie and Worthington sat on the floor. Even through the grime-covered windows, Jennie could see dozens more specters watching from outside.

"Member?" Lupe chuckled. "The Spectral Plane is mine. I own this rowdy rabble of specters!" He laughed loudly. Obscenely, small globs of spit sprayed from his mouth as he turned to the specters, and they laughed in return. "*Incluso en la muerte, los vivos controlan la historia.*"

The specters laughed even harder.

Worthington leaned toward Jennie. "What did he say?"

"Even in death, the living control the story," Jennie told him.

"Very good!" Lupe praised. "You have a good grasp of the Spanish language."

"Thanks. I spent several months over there dealing with a group of specters who were involved in a drug cartel and got far too big for their britches. Spanish isn't too different from any other Indo-European language once you know the basics."

"Spanish is a beautiful language," Lupe crooned. "The language of love. The language of laughter. The language of life."

Jennie gave him a sharp look. "And, now the language of death, it would appear."

"*Bueno.*" Lupe calmed down and stroked his chin, examining the pair in front of him. In the flickering candlelight, his litany of scars and cuts made his face look more gruesome than before, as though *he* had been resurrected. "I have to admit, I am surprised you found me down here. No other mortal has managed to figure out the location of our headquarters."

"Well, you know." Jennie shrugged. "Sniff out a specter, follow the trail. I'm kind of like a bloodhound that way. I'm more surprised that you are the leader of the Spectral Plane. Tell me, how does that work? You make a group of followers in life, and when you die, you've got somewhere to go to? That how it works?"

A smile teased Lupe's lips. "Something like that. As I'm sure you well know. When you're a conduit to the afterlife, anything is possible."

His eyes fixed intensely on Jennie.

Worthington looked confused. "I'm sorry, a 'conduit?'"

"One who can commune and channel the dead," Lupe replied, his eyes not moving from Jennie's. "We are a rare breed, you and I."

"We'll be rarer when I finally commit you to the afterlife," Jennie retorted. "You know we have come straight from the queen, and we intend to shut you down and put an end to all of this nonsense."

Lupe's eyebrows raised. "Nonsense?"

"Too polite?" Jennie continued. "Okay, then, bullshit." She broke Lupe's gaze and addressed the specters crowding around them. "Her Paranormal Majesty, Queen Victoria, has personally sent us to pass on the message that *any* specter plotting against the crown will suffer severe consequences. There is only room in the world for one paranormal power, and the paranormal court has held this post for centuries. Put aside your petty differences and pledge allegiance to the crown if you wish to live. If not, then suffer your exorcism and accustom yourself to the final death. The choice is yours. I will not ask again."

A moment of silence as the specters stared at Jennie. She met their eyes in turn, knowing it wouldn't be as easy as that. Still, she had to at least give everyone the chance to surrender before things got ugly.

Lupe stood up and clapped. "I knew you had big *cojones*, *señorita*. I'd heard the stories about you and your...gifts. But let's be real here. Your queen has overstayed her welcome. New is better." He turned and indicated the crowd of specters around them. "We're armed to the teeth. You've brought yourself and a teeny-tiny specter sporting the clothes of the enemy. I highly recommend you consider your options."

"I did," Jennie replied matter-of-factly. "I made my choice before I entered the underground."

"Subway," Worthington muttered.

"Does it matter?"

Lupe let out a snort of derision. He drew a knife from his side and pointed it at Jennie. "I knew you wouldn't go easily, so I prepared. It's a truth that sometimes you have to cut out a mole to prevent cancer."

Jennie scoffed. "It's a shame that you're stupid enough to think that an itty-bitty knife is going to fix all your problems."

As she finished talking, the two guns at her hips appeared as if from nowhere as the cloak of Worthington's power lifted and allowed them to become visible.

"Fancy weaponry," Lupe admired.

Jennie smirked. "Better than your prick."

Lupe leaped, determined to attack Jennie before she could reach for her guns.

Jennie saw his maneuver coming. Her mind already focused, she reached out and latched on to two nearby specters, dragging them together and causing them to collide in front of her. The specters groaned as they solidified and formed a metaphysical barrier that stopped Lupe from crossing.

Jennie threw the specters and Lupe back against the carriage wall, shattering what was left of the glass from the window.

"Get them!" Lupe shouted before the wind was knocked from his stomach.

Jennie leaped to her feet, now completely surrounded by specters. She reached for Worthington and felt herself become incorporeal as she helped him to his feet and her connection grew stronger by the second. "If you want to fight like a specter, you have to become a specter."

"Way to state the obvious, Jennie," Worthington told her dryly. "But do you have a next step to this plan?"

Jennie grinned. She loved introducing new specters to her arsenal of powers, which was one of the reasons she allowed the queen to assign her new partners. Worthington had experienced some of the tricks in her bag, but there was a lot more hiding inside. "Now I employ the combat skills I learned while training in Thailand back in 1926. Or was it 1936? I forget. At a certain point, the years all become one."

A specter reached for her. She swiveled out of the way, caught the crook of his arm over her shoulder, and pitched him forward. The specter tumbled over her body and disappeared through the carriage floor.

"Lucky son of a bitch. I wish I could do that." She saw her ghostly glow. "Oh, wait. I can." She slipped through the floor as several pairs of hands reached for her and landed next to the wheels of the train.

It was dark on the tracks. Jennie heard the frantic scrabbling above her and knew she had to act fast. The specter she had thrown through the floor was now nearly out of the underbelly of the carriage and gave her a sarcastic wave.

"Jennie?"

Jennie turned to her right at the sound of her name and saw Baxter tied up and strapped to the underbelly of the train. "Baxter?"

"Fancy seeing you here," he remarked.

"What are you doing?" she asked.

The specter she had been chasing scrambled to his feet.

"Hold on." Jennie reached into her pocket and pulled out a

ghostly knife. She quickly slashed the ropes, and Baxter fell the couple of feet to the ground with a gasp.

She turned her attention to the other specter, gesturing with her hands as she reached out with her power. A thin trail of power ran between the pair. Jennie felt the moment her connection captured him.

With a cocky wink, she grabbed the thread and *pulled.*

Jennie launched herself forward at a remarkable speed and tucked her arms tightly at her sides as she propelled herself toward the specter. When she reached him, she grabbed him and the pair went rolling down the ancient tracks until they came to a standstill.

"How the…" the specter coughed.

Jennie straddled him and punched him in the face. "That's what you get when you try to grab me." Another punch. "And *that's* for being a complete wanker."

She turned at the sound of voices.

The specters from the train were outside the carriage and coming for her.

"Watch and learn. You haven't seen the half of it." She smirked, running back toward the throng.

She drew her pistol and the Big Bitch. As she ran, she fired at several specters and shot the cocky grins off their faces.

Panic set in when they realized that somehow, they could be injured by the guns.

Heads splattered as Jennie continued firing, but their bodies remained mobile. Now dozens of specters were walking in circles, bashing into each other.

Realizing there were too many, Jennie twirled the guns around her fingers and slotted them back into the holsters as she reached the throng and the specters came at her with dogged determination on their faces. She blocked several punches with her forearms, and one with her shin as she maneuvered around the group, dodging blows and sending several jabs and uppercuts their way.

Her heart beat fast, and adrenaline flooded her blood. She felt alert and present, able to see all the action taking place around her.

At one point, a woman went for a kick, and Jennie raised her leg just in time to avoid it connecting with her knee. She raised her knee to her chest, then stamped back down, at the same time managing to grab a man's wrist and deflecting his punch, which was aimed straight at her face.

But there were a lot of them, and she was just one woman. After a few minutes of valiant fighting, the specters began to pile on top of her. Soon she was lost beneath a sea of them, all working to compress her and keep her down to stop her from doing damage.

After a few minutes, Jennie went still.

Lupe dabbed the blood which had formed in the corner of his mouth, still unable to understand what had just happened.

He had been a conduit to the specters for as long as he could remember. Could commune with them and see them wandering down the streets since he was a little boy on the borders of Mexico.

Yet, he had never *felt* a specter. In all his fifty years on this Earth, he had never run the risk of a specter *hurting* him. Becoming physical enough to do him damage.

But the specters had *hurt you, hadn't they? Had flown through the air and collided with you like boulders, blasting you back against the carriage walls.*

Lupe rose to his feet and straightened his robes. The specters had jumped in to defend him, so that was good. It was nice to know that even in life, he had earned the respect of the dead.

That his thralls had his back and hadn't been full of shit when they'd pledged their allegiance to him as the leader of the Spectral Plane.

The true *leader. Not like those shitty pretenders up on the surface. The ones who claimed to be clairvoyants and psychics but wouldn't recognize a poltergeist if it fucked them in their sleep.*

He wandered through the train carriage, past the old Englishman who had accompanied the woman. He was bound and held firm by two of his finest men. Lupe worked his way to the back window. His specters were down there now, a huge pile-up of bodies on top of the woman. A heaving mass weighing down upon her, neutralizing the one person he had met who he was sure would ruin his plans for revolution.

"You know she's playing you like a steel drum?" Worthington remarked. "You're playing right into her hands."

"And what do you know of our plan?" Lupe retorted. "The Spectral Plane can shatter the girl with the power of Thor's hammer. If she wants to risk her life and become a specter, then so be it. But she will swear allegiance to me on the other side."

"In your dreams," Worthington told him dryly.

Lupe stared intently at the heaving mass, wondering how long his specters would wait there. He growled as he saw the large black man he had tied under the train emerge and start tossing bodies off the pile.

He was about to shout for someone to get him back under control and tie the specter back up when he felt something change in the air.

The temperature dropped several degrees. A rumble on the subway floor caused dust and debris to fall like snow from the ceiling.

The specters began to murmur and mumble.

"I hate to say I told you so," Worthington managed before one of his captors shoved an ethereal cloth into his mouth.

Lupe stared down at the pile-up, trying to work out what was going on. He heard cries of distress from somewhere deep within the pile, followed by fragments of bright white light bursting out of the center.

The next thing he knew, he could see nothing but bright white light. He shielded his eyes and listened to the cries of alarm from his spectral army.

CHAPTER FOURTEEN

Jennie had them all exactly where she wanted them. She huddled beneath the bodies of the specters. One by one, they had formed a protective cocoon around her.

A cocoon from which I can draw strength, suckers.

She formed connections to as many specters as possible, feeling the ethereal energy flow through her. Over the years, she had tested her limits, sometimes overreaching but always growing. Ever since her first test of strength against a little girl named Annabelle, she had continually expanded on how far she could push herself.

Jennie spoke despite the pressure bearing down on her. "Oh, boys? Are you ready to bow down before a new power?"

The specters within her immediate vicinity gasped, suddenly desperate to leave. They were too far beneath the pile to move.

Jennie grinned. "Here we go…"

She began draining the energy of every specter she had tapped, her eyes closed as she focused and worked to maintain her control. The power began to fill her, coursing through her and heating her blood. She felt herself become strong as the energy worked its way into every fiber of her muscles.

Jennie clenched her fists and gritted her teeth. Her arms were folded, but they wouldn't be for long.

Gasps and cries of alarm came from those who could sense what she was doing. They hurried to scramble away, to no avail.

"Here we go…" Jennie's face was inches from a woman who would clearly rather be anywhere than where she was. Jennie gave her a quick kiss on the cheek. "I'll see you on the other side."

Then came the flash of light, the energy forming itself into a ball of power. Jennie worked her arms free as the energy shot outward, immediately feeling the end of the resistance from the specters. The light exploded from her epicenter and the specters were flung away, each one pinned to the tunnel by the thread of power that connected them to her.

Jennie could finally breathe and was able to see the tunnel once more. Her powers held the specters firm against the walls and ceiling as she slowly rose to her feet. She looked haunting in her spectral form, with her eyes completely white and her hair flowing gently behind her as the unseen power pulsed its energy.

She turned and saw Baxter standing by the front of the train with his mouth open

Inside the train, Lupe stood at the window with a furious yet stunned expression on his face.

"I'm going to break my own rules and ask once more, Lupe," Jennie called. "Surrender your people, or…"

Jennie didn't get a chance to finish before Lupe disappeared from the window.

Jennie sighed. "Son of a bitch."

She disconnected herself from the specters and took off after him. One by one, they all slid back down the walls, a few of them dropping heavily from the ceiling. As they landed, they rubbed their heads and watched Jennie disappear back toward the train, wondering what the hell they'd just encountered.

Jennie felt for Worthington's energy and connected herself to him, so she was able to become incorporeal and jump through the train and onto the carriage floor.

Lupe was now several carriages ahead, running without turning back, occasionally slamming his shoulders into the handrails.

"A little help?" Jennie offered, extending a hand to Worthington. The specters who had been holding him let go without a word and allowed him to be helped to his feet.

"Finally," Worthington grumbled. He glanced at the specters. "I know we're dead, and all, but you could at least clean the detritus out of your fingernails. Nasty stuff."

Jennie laughed and got down to her knees, feeling her muscles tense and coil. She channeled Worthington and imagined herself springing after Lupe and closing the distance in seconds. "Ready?"

"I suppose," the Beefeater agreed. "Will this *hurt—*"

Before he could finish, Jennie felt an explosion of energy. She powered forward as though shot from a catapult. The carriages streamed past her as she closed the gap between her and the conduit. She kept her arms close to her body and saw the man grow closer and closer.

Lupe turned and saw the strange spectral blur coming for him. He held the handrail and gave a hard kick to the carriage door. It buckled on its rusty hinges and fell to the tracks. He jumped off and landed on top of it, then ran through the ancient tunnels and into the dark.

Not on my watch, you piece of shit. Jennie caught up to the door and grasped the handrail, using the momentum to swing out into the tunnel.

When she landed, she ran along to the back end of the train, expecting to have to continue running after the small Mexican man.

She didn't expect to find him already wrestled to the floor, with a large specter straddling his back as he furiously kicked and pounded the tracks.

"You're fast," Jennie praised.

Baxter grinned at her. "You're one to talk. Not every day I see a mortal turned into a speeding bullet."

Jennie winked. "Not every day you meet the queen's secret weapon."

Baxter raised an eyebrow and studied Jennie. "Who did you say you were again?"

Jennie drew the Big Bitch from her hip and strode over to the pair. She held the barrel of the gun to the back of Lupe's neck and half-shrugged. "My friends call me Jennie, but most know me as Rogue."

A flicker of recognition passed over Baxter's face at the code-name. "So, what shall I call you?"

Jennie made a deliberate show of chewing her lip and thinking. "Well, considering you've just helped me capture the head of an organization I've been trying to wrap my head around ever since I've arrived in this city, I'd say you can keep calling me Jennie."

Baxter's shoulders softened. "You got it." He pushed himself off Lupe and stood beside him.

Jennie grabbed the back of Lupe's collar and hauled him to his feet. "But don't get cocky. You wouldn't be the first person to have gone from friend to foe in the snap of my fingers. Stay on my good side, and we won't have any problems."

"You got it," Baxter assured her, the uncertainty returning to his face as he watched Jennie march Lupe back toward the train.

Lupe glared at Jennie from underneath the canopy of his brow. "What the fuck *are* you?"

Jennie deliberated this. The specters of the Spectral Plane were all gathered outside of the train, waiting patiently in reverent quiet while Baxter and Worthington guarded the entrance to the carriage.

"I could be just a friendly neighborhood Spiderman." Jennie grinned. "Or I could be your worst goddamn nightmare. That really depends on your answers to my questions."

Lupe struggled against the rope which bound him and growled.

"Now, tell me, Lupe. What is your issue with the supernatural court? The queen has heard of your ploys in the city and decreed that you and your entire organization are enemies of the crown. What do you have to say for yourself?"

"Fuck the crown!" Lupe spat on the floor. "You and your precious loyalties. You are so close to it that you cannot even see what is going on, can you?"

"See what?" Jennie demanded. "I know I can see my fist finding a nesting place in your face if you don't stop talking in riddles. You may not know this, being only a mortal playing in a specter's world, but the court is the only law when it comes to the paranormal world. The queen is a figure of inspiration and someone who rules with an iron fist. She doesn't take rebellion lightly, or the creation of unlicensed and non-aligned specters."

"I know more than you know." Lupe smirked. "You think it's all the same over here? You travel across the Atlantic and think that the same rules apply in the United States? You must be kidding yourself. The paranormal world is different here. Your queen cannot control us."

Jennie sat back in her chair and crossed her leg, looking remarkably at ease. She held the Big Bitch loosely in her hand, occasionally playing with it to remind Lupe it was still there. "And what is your cause?"

"Freedom," Lupe replied simply. "Freedom from the clutches

of an oppressive tyrant. Freedom from those loyal to her who take the city's dirtiest scum and employ them to her purpose. Freedom from the final death for all specters."

For the first time since Baxter had captured Lupe, slight doubt flickered across Jennie's face. "And who are these scum you seem so eager to quash?"

Now Lupe's smile grew. The insides of his teeth were black, his eyes cold. "You really have no idea, do you?"

Jennie gave Lupe an "I'm waiting" look, but it only made him laugh harder.

Jennie turned to Worthington and Baxter. "I'm losing my patience."

Worthington held up a fist in solidarity, while Baxter muttered, "Just shoot him."

Liking Baxter's idea, Jennie lifted the Big Bitch and pulled the trigger. The report was incredible, shattering what little remained of the carriage glass.

Lupe screamed and clapped his hands to his face as dust rained down on them. The specters gasped.

Jennie smelt the tell-tale scent of urine as Lupe's robe darkened around his crotch.

"Packs quite a punch, doesn't it?" Jennie asked, admiring the hole the gun had made in the side of the train. "Imagine that happening to your face."

Lupe took a few steadying breaths, his demeanor changing entirely. "I'm sorry, I'm sorry, I don't want to die, please, no! *Padre nuestro que estás en los cielos, santificado sea tu nombre...*"

"What's he saying?" Worthington asked.

Jennie sighed. "It's the Lord's prayer." She moved forward until she was nose to nose with Lupe. Her stare was intense, drilling into his very soul.

She brought the Big Bitch up and stroked his chin with the barrel. "Start talking. Now."

"Okay, okay, okay!" he whimpered. "I never meant for it to get so out of hand, okay? I thought I was doing the world a favor. Finding a way to use my gift for good. Tanya and the others, they *believed*. They needed me to help them, so I did."

Lupe told Jennie and the others about how he had accidentally stumbled upon his gift a few years ago and couldn't quite believe what was happening. He was able to speak to and see specters wandering around the city, and it wasn't until he started engaging in conversations that he learned of the paranormal court and the power of Queen Victoria.

"I respected it at first. Thought that the Winter Court was a place to be revered, a place of loyalty and honesty, but then darkness began to creep through the city."

Jennie allowed an oversight at Lupe's use of "Winter Court."

Lupe and some of the neutrals began to hear stories of a darker force in the city. A group of specters who had taken to employing the scum of the city and amassing a small army behind them. For several months, neutrals had been going missing, and some had borne witness to exorcisms of their friends by a rogue group proclaiming to be aligned with the paranormal court.

"There was a conflict," Lupe continued. "A month or so ago, our people met them out in the streets. They were relentless, but they were a small group, and luckily, our numbers were greater. We pushed them back into the hole they crawled out of and they have been quiet ever since."

Lupe looked at his feet. "We don't know where they went or when they'll come back again. All we know is that there is corruption in the crown, and we are gathering so that we can break what has been spawned."

When Lupe fell quiet, Jennie took a moment to think. The whole idea seemed ludicrous. The paranormal court was an honest power who had treated her and the others with nothing more than civility and respect.

So why would Lupe lie? Most rebellion forces are born out of a genuine cause, whether that's intolerance, racism, or fear, and she could definitely tell that there was a modicum of fear in each and every specter gathered around them.

None of this makes any sense.

"Why should I believe you?" Jennie asked at last, moving her gun back to Lupe's chin. "What possible reason would I have to doubt the crown?"

"Because we've seen them," a voice shouted from outside of the train.

Jennie rose, moved between Worthington and Baxter, and looked down at a woman in a spectral set of silk pajamas. "Excuse me?"

"We were there," another specter called. "We battled the crown, and we lived to tell the tale."

Worthington's eyes darted around the crowd as more specters took a step forward, confirming the story. "Don't listen to them, Jennie. It could be a trap."

Jennie nodded gently. "Or it could be the truth," she whispered. "I've seen a lot of liars in my time, and I know what that face looks like. Whether or not they're misguided, these specters genuinely believe the crown is out to get them."

"But just *think* of what they're suggesting," Worthington urged. "To doubt the crown is treason."

"Only when you've pledged your oath," Jennie replied. "None of these specters owe anything to the crown. All they've known is neutrality and the Spectral Plane."

Lupe interrupted their bickering. "I think I may be able to prove that what I'm saying is true."

Jennie's eyes narrowed. "Let me guess. In exchange, I have to cut your bonds and set you free."

Lupe shrugged. "From one conduit to another, I swear this is no trick."

Jennie grimaced. "I'm no conduit, and I'm tired of all these oaths." She reached down and cut Lupe free. "Guide me out of these rat tunnels and show me what you know."

Lupe rubbed his wrists and nodded. "You will not be disappointed. Soon, even you may see the truth behind the Winter Court's veil."

CHAPTER FIFTEEN

<u>New York City, USA, Present Day</u>

Jennie raised a hand to shield her eyes as they exited the subway station.

After leaving the abandoned passageways, the underground tunnels had been a lot busier than when they had gone down in the first place. It was now morning, which meant rush-hour commuters. As they climbed onto the subway platform, several men and women in pristine suits and holding briefcases muttered behind their hands and scoffed at their colleagues.

Jennie ignored them all, keeping Lupe at arm's length in front of her. At his request, a pair of Spectral Plane specters trailed behind them, their eyes fixed on Worthington and Baxter.

As they had walked through the tunnel, Lupe had told them how he had never meant to get caught up in a feud between two spectral parties. At first, he had simply used his gift to gather knowledge from the dead, but after learning about oaths and experimenting with them, he had learned that he could assign specters to himself.

"Why hide them from the mortals in the Spectral Plane?"

Jennie had asked. "It would've made Tanya's day to know your plans were working."

"I wanted to keep them out of danger," he replied, squeezing through the turnstiles and out toward the stairs. "The more I learned about the Winter Court and their schemes, the more I knew I had to protect them. They helped me build my army, so at least I could keep them out of harm's way."

"Would you *please* stop disrespecting Her Majesty?" Worthington huffed, glaring at Lupe. "She can hear, you know. She has abilities beyond anything you could conceive."

Jennie arched an eyebrow. *He must be talking about a different queen.*

The sun was rising above the skyscrapers. It was another cloudless blue day. Jennie ignored the strange looks that she and Lupe got as he led her through the streets and away from the main hub of activity in the city.

He took a left at the intersection, and they paused at the crossing. A red hand told pedestrians to wait. Baxter whistled and looked around the people waiting to cross. "I really need to come out in the daytime more. I forget how interesting people are."

The woman he stood inside shivered and adjusted her shawl.

A car horn blared as a man with slicked-back hair and a stylish goatee sprinted across the road.

"I guess someone has a wish to join the spectral side sooner than most," Worthington side-mouthed. "Think we can get him to take his oath now?"

Jennie chuckled. Lupe glared at him.

As the lights changed, Jennie heard an engine revving. A red Ford Mustang Ecoboost sat with its engine idling as the driver, a man who looked like he was in the middle of his midlife crisis, belted out the middle section of Queen's *Bohemian Rhapsody*, clearly unaware that his car wasn't soundproof and several pedestrians were laughing as his voice went high and low to match Freddie Mercury's.

Jennie whistled, pulling down her glasses to the bridge of her nose to get a look at the car. "Da-*yum*, that's a pretty ride."

The man stared out of his windscreen and saw Jennie looking his way. He grinned, wound his window down, and put his elbow on the sill. "Hey, pretty lady. Wanna ride? You can hop in the car for a spin after if you like."

Jennie pushed her glasses back and smirked at his left hand, which rested atop his steering wheel. He had a silver band on his third finger. "I'm sure your wife would *love* that, wouldn't she?" She crossed the street without another glance at him.

The man blushed as several pedestrians sniggered and glanced his way.

Jennie continued to the other side of the road, sparing one last look at the car. The pedestrian lights turned red before the Mustang revved and screeched around the corner.

She made a mental note that should her visit to New York extend past its planned date, she'd explore options for vehicles.

Lupe led Jennie toward Lower Manhattan, once more weaving between the thin, shadowed alleys between the blocks. Jennie caught sight of several rats and alley cats among the dumpsters and trash and found herself sighing at several homeless people nestled up and fast asleep in the dirt.

A short while later, Lupe reached the mouth of an alley and paused. He waved an arm and motioned them ahead. "Here. Go ahead and find your proof."

Jennie nodded for Worthington and Baxter to guard Lupe while she went ahead. The alley was wider than some of the others, with several back doors that opened into a mix of international-inspired restaurants and diners. Jennie took a step back and looked up at the wall.

A large spray of crude graffiti covered the wall's surface. The paint was a dark crimson that looked like blood, and in the places where the letters curved and joined, blots of paint had dripped down the wall.

Jennie's stomach tightened. The words read, "Long live the paranormal court. Kill the revolters," and were finished off with what could only be described as a child's drawing of Queen Victoria's crown.

Revolters?

Jennie searched her mind, wondering what this could mean. She had never experienced anything like it. Specters had always been secretive about their work and life beyond death. Nearly all specters liked the secrecy their new life brought. Aside from poltergeists, mortals hardly ever came into contact with the denizens of the afterlife.

"Well?" Worthington called from down the alley. "Have you found anything?"

Jennie took a breath and beckoned them all toward her. Baxter and Worthington remained behind Lupe as he walked over to the art. Lupe's personal specters seemed hardly to notice, while Worthington and Baxter groaned.

"Well, that's not good," Baxter grumbled.

"Not good?" Worthington looked fit to burst. "Do you realize what this is? This is blasphemy. This is treason. This is…"

He whirled on Lupe. "This is *your* doing. You're planting ideas in her head, aren't you? Defaming the prestige of the one true ruler of the paranormal for the sake of your rebellion."

Lupe shook his head, eyes wide. "No, I did not. What possible reason would I have to paint this? You think I planned this? Made a backup plan in case the woman who was trampling around New York caught us, and I needed to trick her? What kind of pre-planning would that take?"

"Something stinks," Worthington insisted.

"We are standing by trash," Baxter replied.

Worthington ignored his comment and turned to Jennie. "You don't believe this nonsense, do you? The Spectral Plane is the *enemy*, and they're feeding us this bullshit like it's going out of date. Give them a few more days, and they'll have you convinced that our queen tricked us all into slavery, and the world is nothing more than her plaything."

Jennie scratched her chin, deep in thought.

Lupe took a tentative step forward. "Look, I know that this may all seem hard to believe, particularly for representatives of the crown. But what possible reason would we have to lie to you?"

"Because you're in the presence of Rogue and know that she'll exorcise you as soon as look at you all?" Worthington glared. "What better way to win your fight than drawing the queen's allies to your side?"

Baxter nodded. "Your boy's got a point."

"Enough!" Jennie's eyes were dark. "Worthington, you are right. There's no better way to win a fight than to sow the seeds of doubt in your enemy's closest advisors—"

"Thank you."

She lifted a hand. "But still, something doesn't add up here. If there were recruiters for the crown working to bring all the scum and dirtbags in the city to their side, surely we'd know about it? We'd have seen them, or the queen would have made us aware? There isn't a place where she doesn't have eyes."

"If I may...?"

The smaller of Lupe's two specters raised a hand and sheepishly stood forward. He looked to be no more than sixteen years old, but his arms were thick with muscle, and his outfit suggested he had been lifted straight out of the 1700s.

"Yes?"

"You've said it yourself. New York is miles from your home. Can you honestly say that you think your queen knows *everything* that goes on around here? Can you say with your hand on your heart that there isn't even the smallest of chances that a small faction of those loyal to the crown could have gone rogue and are now trying to work the city using her name?"

Worthington shook his head and scowled but remained quiet.

Baxter looked at the Spectral Plane specters and Jennie as though watching a tennis match.

Jennie took a long breath and squared her shoulders. "I'm inclined to say that I hope for their sakes there isn't such a party in the city. There's only room in this world for one Rogue, and this bitch has already taken that role."

CHAPTER SIXTEEN

The Plaza, New York City, Present Day

"I can't believe you let them go," Worthington muttered as they arrived back in Jennie's suite at The Plaza. "No reprimand. Nothing. Just free."

"Whatever happened to innocent until proven guilty?" Jennie replied, heading for the minibar and pulling out a variety of bottles.

"They confessed to rallying a rebellious force to take down our Paranormal Majesty, Queen Victoria!" Worthington shouted. "Case closed! Drag them over the coals and put an end to this madness."

Jennie stood up and twisted off lids to several juices and liquors while Baxter wandered over to the window and looked out at the view. It was midday in the city, and the streets below were throbbing with road and foot traffic. Birds flew low over Central Park, and people could be seen milling about the paths and trees, likely city employees wanting to take a few moments to connect with nature on their lunch breaks.

"That's a hell of a view," Baxter marveled.

"Thanks," Jennie told him.

Worthington's eyes looked fit to pop. "Are you even listening to me right now?" He marched over to Jennie and slapped his hands on the counter. "Your job is to remove the rebellion, and there you were with the whole group in your grasp. Why didn't you do something? *Anything?*"

"What would you have had me do?" Jennie asked, her voice calm and measured. She crouched to be at eye level with a measuring cup and began pouring in her ingredients. "Blasted them with the Big Bitch and sent a message to them all? Performed a mass exorcism and sent them all to the abyss?"

Baxter turned, his eyebrows raised. "You can do that?"

Jennie shook her head, not taking her eyes off her mixture. She now had half a cocktail shaker filled with a light pink liquid that foamed at the top. "Afraid not. Nice to know you thought I could, though."

Baxter shrugged. "After everything I saw last night, there's nothing I won't believe you can't do."

Jennie smiled, finally looking up from her drink and meeting Baxter's eyes. "You're making me blush."

Worthington's fists shook. "They've got you, haven't they? You genuinely believe those *traitors*, don't you?" He marched around the counter until he was next to Jennie, head angled over her shoulder. "You know the queen won't take kindly to lapses in loyalty, don't you? You know that once you've sworn your oath, you're bound to her, and the only way out is death."

Jennie stuck a lid on her cocktail and began to shake. She deliberately shook it over her shoulder where Worthington's head had been, forcing him to step back. "And is that death with a side of chips or salad?"

Baxter and Jennie scoffed.

"What are you laughing at, *neutral?*" Worthington spat the word as though it were a curse word. "You can have an opinion when you pick your allegiance."

Baxter strode across the room and stood in front of Worthington with his hands on his hips. Standing straight, he was far taller than Worthington; the top of the Beefeater's hat was only just higher than the crown of Baxter's head. "You want to say that again, short stuff?"

Worthington puffed out his chest. "Just try me."

Jennie rolled her eyes and set down three martini glasses. She popped the lid of the metal shaker and poured a healthy measure into each.

The scent of fresh juices and berries met her nostrils. The liquid was milkshake-pink and thick with a thin layer of white foam on top. Small particles of dark red floated inside. She finished the drink with a dash of milk, sending the pinks into dirty swirls.

After she added the final touches—half a strawberry over the rim of the glass and a sprinkling of sugar—she pushed two of the glasses toward the specters and raised her own to her lips.

"Ah!" she exclaimed appreciatively. "That's good stuff. Now, how about you two break it up and try these bad boys before I drink them all myself?"

Worthington took a step back, clearly glad of an excuse to get out from under Baxter's shadow.

"What is it?"

"As my old buddy Hendrix would call it, 'A Flamboyant Flamingo.' Not that that's what I've come to call it over the years."

"What do you call it?" Worthington asked, his intrigue overtaking his anger.

Jennie grinned devilishly. "A burst testicle."

Worthington huffed.

Baxter scoffed. "Wait a minute, did you say Hendrix? As in, *Jimmy* Hendrix?"

"What?" Jennie replied, a pink mustache on her face from drinking her cocktail. "Oh, no. Brunhilde Hendrix. A woman I met in Germany. Couldn't play a lick like Jimmy, but she could run the track. Great over short distances. Big fan of the cocktails, too, which I never understood, given that her instructor was pretty strict with her diet plan." She took another sip. "Ah, well, times were different back then. Come, drink up."

Worthington eyed Jennie. "You know we can't."

"Oh, that's *right!*" She slapped her head theatrically. "You're not mortal, so you can't drink the drink. Can you at least smell it?"

Baxter took a deep sniff. "*I* can. Not sure about mince-muncher here."

"It's *Beefeater,*" Worthington snapped. He waved his arms. "Why are we discussing cocktails?"

"Burst testicles," Jennie corrected.

Worthington gave her an icy look. "We *should* be wrangling the enemy. When I tell the queen about this…" His voice trailed off, and he took a seat on the armchair and crossed his arms.

"Oh, relax, Worthington." Jennie grinned. "Why do you think I'm making these delicious drinks?"

"Because you're a booze-addled buffoon?" Worthington immediately regretted his words.

Jennie shot him a look. "Because I work better when I'm relaxed, and what's more relaxing than fresh fruit juice mixed with just a dash of vodka and Triple Sec?"

"A dash?" Baxter asked.

"Okay, a quart." Jennie laughed. "Look, the answer here is simple. We have two options. Numero one, we call up Queen Vicky, give her the LD on what we've discovered so far, and find out if she knows anything about this corruption in the city."

Worthington looked puzzled. "'LD?'"

"Lowdown," Baxter told him.

"Do *not* call her 'Vicky,'" Worthington ordered. "You've gotten into trouble for that before."

Jennie nodded, lost in memory. "You'd think that after a hundred and twenty years in the paranormal world she would have moved on with the times. 'Vicky' is much trendier."

Worthington sighed. "Admittedly, it is a much better nickname than 'V-dawg.'"

"*That* did not go down well," Jennie agreed. "I wasn't allowed near Her Royal Highness for a week. They took me off all cases until I'd had 'adequate time to atone for my uncontrollable tongue.'"

"How long did that last?" Baxter asked, sticking his hands in his pockets.

"About two days," Jennie told him. "A poltergeist managed to get hold of an unlicensed firearm in Lisbon, and they needed someone to put an end to his rampage." She brushed a hand over her hair. "When a job needs doing, this bitch gets it done."

"Speaking of which," Worthington reminded her. "What's option number two?"

Jennie grinned. "We keep our findings thus far quiet from Her Majesty, and we go and seek out this rogue group of the queen's army. Personally, that's the one I favor."

Worthington shifted uncomfortably. "Keep a secret from the queen? But...that's against the rules. She won't like that one bit. It's already been several days, and we've not even called to let her know how we're getting on."

"She's a big girl; she can survive without us for a little while," Jennie told him. She turned to Baxter. "What do you think, big guy? Phone it in or go undercover?"

Baxter shrugged. "I'm not sure it counts as going undercover, but I'm in for an adventure if you guys'll have me."

Jennie looked at Worthington for approval.

He shook his head. "No. No way. Nope."

Jennie clapped her hands. "He's in!"

As Worthington scowled, Jennie drained the other two drinks she had made. She patted her stomach and placed the glass back down, hiding a small belch behind her fist. "Okay, troops. I highly advise we rest up and get ready for a fun night ahead. The minute the sunlight kisses the horizon, we're going to take to the streets to find these renegades. Who's with me?"

Jennie winked when they looked at her blankly. "*Carpe noctem?*"

"*Carpe noctem!*" Baxter replied.

Worthington hesitated. "If this is the path we're choosing, why don't we just get on our way and find the culprits?"

There was a slight slur to Jennie's words. She wiped her lips with the back of her hand. "Because we mortals don't have the energy you specters do, particularly after we just spent the whole evening traipsing through the subway and using my energy to kick an entire organization into gear." She stared longingly at the empty glasses. "Besides, that vodka is already kicking in, and if I don't find a comfortable bed to sleep in, I might end up doing something I regret."

"Like what?" Baxter asked eagerly.

Worthington hushed Jennie before she could reply. "Don't tug that thread. You don't know this woman as well as I do."

"Agreed," Baxter replied. "But I like her already."

Jennie slept soundly in her bed as the bustling city went about its daily cycle. With the curtains drawn and the door closed, it could easily have been nighttime.

Time was irrelevant, a fleeting abstract concept that passed her by as she snoozed. In another room, Baxter closed his eyes and feigned his own rest.

She dreamed of many things, as she always did. Her mind fluttered about its resting cycles and blurred memories with imagination in dreams of times long since passed. Oftentimes these were happy memories. Theaters she'd visited across the world, celebrities she'd met, people she'd saved.

But sometimes, on rare occasions, the dreams turned sour and began to melt down the blackboard like liquid chalk.

Jennie's eyes blinked rapidly beneath their lids.

The year was 1943, the location northern France. Jennie was surrounded on all sides by men dressed in military uniforms, eyes to the scopes of their weaponry as they fired out of the trenches and across the no man's land in between them and the enemy.

Wind gusts kicked up thick billows of dust, clouding the land. Mines and bombs shattered eardrums and sent great chunks of dirt exploding in all directions.

"Really makes your dick hard, doesn't it?" Sergeant Liam Keelan grinned as he tugged on his groin and winked at his comrade.

Jennie's lip curled in disgust.

"Are they all like this?" she asked.

Harrington Tinkleman, her specter, had been a military pilot shot down while flying over Switzerland during World War I.

He stood next to her now, his pilot goggles tight about his head, his leathers covering his body, and a thick white mustache from beneath which he spoke. "You get used to it. They're all bloody animals. No women around and long hours firing at men can do funny things to the brain."

Jennie could see how humor got them through it. "Were you ever like that?"

Harrington gave a chesty laugh. "Are you kidding me? I was the worst among the fleet. How do you think I got the nickname 'Tallywhacker Tinkleman?'"

Jennie gave him a look, then peered back over the battlefield. Soon they would come, and while the mortals battled each other, the specters would fall into her trap.

Bullets whizzed through Jennie's spectral form, maintained by her connection to Harrington. Soon enough, she saw the spectral glow. Dozens of poltergeists dashed toward the men in the trenches, rebels from the other side, whose only goal was to distract and destroy the queen's efforts to aid the living.

They were haunting in spectral form, with eyes that were no

more than white dots in their faces. Yet they appeared as less than faint wisps of light to the mortal eye.

Jennie whipped out the Big Bitch and began firing, her teeth bared as she and Harrington charged. Her hands moved quickly, taking them down with unrivaled ease. She laid dozens of poltergeists out cold in the mud, their bodies losing their luster as they worked to heal from their wounds.

In the heartbeat Jennie watched them, the mortals charged across the fields, guns blazing. Men were getting shot and taken down from both sides.

Jennie's heart ached for the men she had grown to know, even if they would never know her. These men were dying to protect the crown in life. To protect George VI and everything the British monarchy held dear.

Jennie shut off her connection to Harrington, ignoring his cries. She solidified and let her bullets fly in the faces of the enemy, tearing them down by the dozen as she screamed and shouted and raged.

The men in the trenches held fire as their attention was captivated by the beautiful stranger with guns that never stopped firing.

She could hear them as she snoozed in her bed. The reports were as loud as thunder, the cries harrowing and close. A lot of bloodshed for the sake of freedom, and this was where it all ended up. Over seventy years later, and the friction and the fighting never ceased.

She saw him running toward her—the last man she would murder in cold blood during the great wars, eyes wide, his dirty face streaked with tears as he ate the metal of her bullets.

He fell with his comrades, his trigger finger still clenched.

Jennie woke with a start, her forehead peppered with sweat. For a fleeting moment, she could hear them all. Could still see it in the ghostly veil behind her eyelids.

And then she heard someone talking. Worthington.

She flopped her head back on the pillow and felt the dampness of her sheets. She didn't often have bad dreams, but when she did, they were vivid enough to carry her back in time. She stared into the darkness and saw the LED of the alarm clock beside her blink 5:43 pm.

With a grunt, she rose from her bed and put on a plain white t-shirt and a pair of khaki trousers. She pawed at her eyes and left her bedroom.

She was violated by the setting sun as it made its slow descent over the park. The golden rays sliced through the window, their warmth causing her to sweat. She looked around the apartment but saw neither Baxter nor Worthington.

Not a surprise, really, she thought. *It's not like those two had much in common or got along.*

Still, she poked her head around the other rooms and looked for her two spectral buddies.

Neither of them was in sight.

She shrugged, wandered over to the minibar, and pulled out two bottles from the fridge. She held them up, debating what to make next. On the left was orange juice and on the right passionfruit.

She knew from her years of study of foods, drinks, and cocktail ingredients that orange juice would hold the greatest amount of nutrients to build effective immunity against earthly illnesses.

On the other hand, passionfruit is fucking delicious.

Jennie decided on passionfruit and poured herself a glass. She downed it in one gulp and was about to refill the glass when she heard mumbling out in the corridor.

Jennie looked down at her hips and realized she had left her guns in her room.

No matter, she thought, trying to think of the last time someone had managed to get a good shot at her before she killed them. Her guns were certainly helpful in battle, but they weren't entirely necessary, not when she'd had over a century to study martial arts.

She tiptoed to the door and poked her head around the doorframe. She could hear someone speaking somewhere down the hall in a hushed voice. There were hurried whispers and momentary silences.

Jennie crept down the hall, fists clenched and ready for anyone who might suddenly leap out and attack.

No one came.

She reached a T intersection at the end of the corridor and paused. She could hear the voice clearly now—an English accent talking to someone in whispers.

Have Worthington and Baxter settled their differences? She thought maybe they had—until she heard Worthington speak.

"It's not my fault. A thousand apologies, I swear, I can rectify this."

Jennie's eyebrow arched. When had Worthington gotten hold of a cell phone? She knew specters could hack into the network signals and reach long distances, but where had he gotten the cell? Had he stolen it from a neighboring room?

More importantly, what was he apologizing for? Who was he speaking to in that hushed tone?

"Absolutely. No, I completely understand. I will not fail you again." A pause. "Understood. One chance. I can pull her off the scent, I know I can."

Pull her off the scent? What am I, a Labrador?

"I'll call you tomorrow with a full update and report." He paused once more and pinched his eyes. "Yes. I won't let you down, Your Majesty."

Your Majesty? Jennie thought, a scowl appearing on her face. *What in the name of the paranormal court have I stumbled upon?*

CHAPTER SEVENTEEN

Jennie's mind whirled. Something was going on here, and she had to figure it out.

After overhearing the conversation between Worthington and the queen, Jennie tiptoed rapidly back to the apartment and tucked herself back in bed. She heard Worthington sigh as he came back in and shut the door behind him before retiring to the armchair to watch the sun set.

Jennie waited a few minutes before stepping out of her bed once more and emerging into the central living area. She pawed her eyes and stretched. "Still up?"

"You know specters. We don't sleep. Not really," Worthington replied as casually as if nothing had happened.

"Where's Baxter?" she asked.

Worthington shrugged. "Probably downstairs inspecting the hotel's backup generator and marveling at it."

Jennie scratched her chin. "Strange."

"What's that?"

"Well, it's just I thought I heard voices. People talking."

Worthington stiffened and turned his eyes toward the window. "Really? I didn't hear anything."

So, you're going to play it that way, huh?

Jennie nodded silently, returned to her room, and prepared for a busy night.

They found Baxter waiting downstairs in the street, one foot behind him as he rested against the front wall of the Plaza. The concierge stood patiently waiting to greet the guests of the hotel, unaware of the large man watching him with a keen glint in his eye.

"What a shit job," Baxter muttered as Jennie collected him and began to walk down the street. "Standing there for hours on end, being a grunt for the rich and famous."

"I can empathize with that," Worthington grumbled, eyes darting to the back of Jennie's head.

Jennie chose to ignore the comment, slowly turning her thoughts over in her head. Her mind was a muddle of contradictions, and if there was one thing that annoyed Jennie more than scumbags and badly mixed drinks, it was the absence of a clear head.

The answer was out here somewhere. It was all connected, that much she knew. The Spectral Plane, the rogue faction of the crown, the conversation between Worthington and the queen. There had to be a link somewhere, and dammit, if she didn't find it before the night was over, she'd phone in her resignation, pack her bags, and head to some part of the world the queen would never think to look for her.

"Where did you go?" Jennie asked Baxter as they turned south and began to head back toward the source of the graffiti. "I thought you'd abandoned us."

"Abandon you?" Baxter laughed. "Are you kidding? This is the most excitement I've had since I died. No, I couldn't stand being stuck in the apartment with…" He placed his hand to the side of his mouth and thumbed at Worthington. *You-know-who.* So, I went for a walk. Figured I might find out something useful."

Worthington's forehead creased. "Excuse me?"

"Did you discover anything useful?" Jennie asked.

"Not at first. But then I found myself in the Plaza lobby watching that small TV that sits above the bar—you know the ones that are always on silent but have subtitles for loners who want to just sit and have a drink?"

"I know the type."

"Turns out the feud might be going a little more public than some of the specters originally thought. They had a news reporter doing the rounds in Lower Manhattan and on the Upper East Side, showing the tags the specters have been spraying on walls. Looks like the Upper East Side is getting a good display of paint from the Spectral Plane, while Lower Manhattan has had messages sprayed supporting the crown."

Jennie rubbed a hand down her face. "This is getting ridiculous. Why would specters want to draw attention to themselves?"

"It's just a little bit of paint." Worthington scoffed. "We don't even know that the people spraying it are part of the paranormal court. I'm telling you, it's the Spectral Plane trying to mess with our heads. Let's just head down to the subway, round them up, and then head on home. No harm, no foul. Job done."

Jennie gave him a look. "Why would the Spectral Plane paint messages in favor of the queen? To draw attention to themselves?"

"We don't even know it was painted by specters!" Worthington retorted. "Lower Manhattan is a breeding ground for hip-hop. Maybe some young rap artist has somehow caught wind of it and unconsciously named his latest album after something he overheard? I'm telling you, we're wasting our time going to re-investigate."

Jennie whirled on Worthington. Across the street, a group of guys in their mid-twenties wearing suits burst into laughter, clearly inebriated beyond measure. Jennie spied a slightly portly man at the front who wore a gold crown and held a scepter.

Worthington pointed their way. "See? It could even have been those guys."

"That's a bachelor party." Baxter looked at Worthington as though he had several screws loose. "Are you okay, steak-muncher?"

"*Beefeater!*"

"That's what I said." Baxter smirked.

Jennie placed a hand on her hip and took off her glasses. "You seem awfully certain who the culprits of this graffiti are, Worthington. Is there something you're not telling us?"

Worthington struggled to meet Jennie's eyes. "No. No, it's just, I'm sure the queen is worried about how the mission is going is all. I promised her a speedy response."

"You promised her?" Jennie repeated. "Have you spoken to her recently, then?"

Worthington's lips tightened. "No, but I know her, and she doesn't like to be kept waiting."

Jennie turned a searching look on Worthington. "*I've* known her for over half a century longer than you. *She* knew me for years before you were even born. I think the queen will be just fine with me handling my business the way that I always do, and that's getting to the real truth behind the shit. Nine times out of ten, the crimes I'm sent in to solve are not the ones that are visible." She squared up to Worthington. When she spoke, it was deliberate and clear. "I'm just like a bloodhound. Once I catch the scent of truth, I just can't let it go until I've caught that son-of-a-bitch between my teeth."

Worthington gulped.

"Er, Jennie?"

Jennie's eyes remained fixed on Worthington's for a moment longer, wondering if he had pulled the subtext from her words. He wouldn't be the first specter she had scared from their post, and he certainly wouldn't be the last.

"Jennie?"

Jennie tore her eyes away from Worthington. "What is it?"

Baxter stood at the mouth of the alley and pointed to where bright crimson paint splattered the walls.

At least, she hoped it was paint.

Jennie took a step into the alley and saw the lettering—another message on behalf of the crown. This one read, Her legacy will live forever. Stand down or die.

"They're very succinct, aren't they?" she muttered.

Baxter nodded and walked over to the wall. He ran a hand across the words, leaving a red smudge behind. "It's fresh, too. Whoever did this can't be far from here."

Jennie knelt and pulled a small pouch from a pocket on her thigh. There were a number of potions and various concoctions nestled in each pocket.

"What's that?" Baxter asked.

"You'll see." Jennie held a small vial in front of her face and checked that the inside was filled with a liquid the color of the ocean. She unscrewed the lid and threw the liquid into the air.

The minute it left the vial, the liquid expanded at a rapid pace, converting to a gas as it mixed with the oxygen in the air. A great blue cloud billowed around them, flowing with the wind through the alley.

After a few seconds, the gas began to dilute, changing from cobalt to a pale color they could see through. In the midst of the cloud, they saw the outlines of spectral shapes, as if the specters who had been there had left a ghostly trail of breadcrumbs behind.

Baxter breathed in awe. "Impossible."

"Nothing is impossible when you know the secrets of life and death," Jennie murmured. She pocketed the vial and followed the trail through the alley.

Baxter caught up with her and stared down at her pockets. "Do you always carry those with you?"

"Yep." She held up a hand. "Scout's Creed. Always be prepared."

"But I saw you fall in the subway," Baxter remarked. "Aren't you worried about them breaking?"

Jennie chuckled. She withdrew the vial and tossed it casually to Baxter. "Plastic vials. After all, we are in the twenty-first century. The time of glass has long since passed, particularly when you're in my line of business."

Baxter hadn't considered working for the queen as a job. "What exactly *is* your line of business?"

Jennie chewed on this. "Justice, I suppose."

Worthington ran up behind the pair, muttering to himself. He looked at the ghostly shapes they followed with fear flickering over his features.

The shapes led them to the end of the alley and back into the street. The farther they went, the harder it was to pick up the trail. Jennie wasn't worried. If she knew specters as well as she thought she did, there'd be another clue soon enough.

She was right. Just as they thought they'd reached the end of the trail and found themselves in another empty alley, Baxter fell to one knee and touched the ground.

"Paint?" He raised a red finger and showed the others.

"Or blood," Worthington argued. "Likely the Spectral Plane getting ready to kill their next victims."

"Ghosts don't bleed," Jennie retorted. "Or, if they do, I'm yet to find a way to make it happen."

The red dots of paint led farther into the alley. Jennie raised her head and saw with surprise, that they were back in the alley they had been in the previous night. The smell of Indian and Thai food spilled from the open doorways at the backs of the restaurants and filled their nostrils. From inside, they could hear the sounds of enthusiastic diners and authoritative chefs.

And somewhere nearby, a man begging for his life.

CHAPTER EIGHTEEN

"Please, don't make me do this…"

Jennie's ears pricked up. Without thinking, she drew her guns and tiptoed farther down the alley.

"From the look of things, you don't have too much of a choice, darling. Either you bow your head and accept what's coming to you, or we'll find a way to splatter your brains on this fucking wall and use the blood to decorate this shit-tunnel."

Jennie's brow creased. It was a man talking, a man with a slight accent she couldn't quite place.

"I'd take his advice if I were you," a woman cut in. "He doesn't mess around. Believe me, I've seen what he's capable of."

Jennie nodded for the other two to join her. Baxter gave a nod, a determined expression on his face as he drew his own gun and moved behind Jennie. Worthington took the back of the line, his head resting against the wall as he closed his eyes and breathed heavily.

Jennie chanced a peek around the corner and couldn't believe what she saw.

Pinstripe and Frock were back, only this time they were no longer afraid of being trapped by Lupe and his Spectral Plane gang in Central Park. It seemed as if freedom agreed with them since they now held a poor spectral woman up against the wall.

Pinstripe's Tommy gun was aimed at her face, while Frock fanned herself with her parasol. Behind them were several tins of red paint.

"So, what's it going to be, darling? The choice is yours."

The woman cringed from the gun. "Please, I don't want to take sides in this petty feud. I've been a neutral for the best part of forty years, and I intend to stay that way. Fighting only ends in pain, and I'm not about to inflict that on someone else. I've seen what you shit-stains do."

Pinstripe's face darkened. He looked at the ground, shook his head, and scoffed. "Oh, dear, dear, dear. I thought you'd be smarter than that." He turned to Frock. "Put your umbrella up, dollface. It's about to rain blood in this alley."

Frock obeyed, tucking herself neatly behind the parasol.

Pinstripe laughed, his hands tightening on the gun.

The woman closed her eyes and screamed, prepared for the worst.

Before he squeezed the trigger, however, another shot was fired from nearby. Pinstripe yelled in surprise as his gun flew out of his hands and clattered to the ground several meters away.

Jennie ran toward Pinstripe with both guns trained on him. Baxter loomed behind her with his weapon aimed at Frock.

Pinstripe shook his hands in reaction to the impact of Jennie's bullet knocking the gun out of them.

The woman they'd been holding against her will groaned and took the opportunity to slip through the wall and away from the conflict.

"I wondered if I'd be seeing you two again." Jennie smirked. "Don't worry, you'll get better with your gun again. I mean, you were trapped in that rock for years, right? You must be a little rusty."

Pinstripe's expression morphed from shock to grim satisfaction. "Not too rusty to obey orders and lure the fabled Rogue out of hiding."

Jennie cocked an eyebrow. "You know my name? Well, that saves introductions."

"Well, that and the fact that you'll soon be dead." Frock giggled. "You're a mortal playing in the specters' world. How long do you think that'll last?"

Jennie began counting on her fingers. "Let's see. Yesterday was Tuesday, so that would make it…" She lowered her fingers and raised her gun again. "Nearly a hundred and forty years, bitch."

Frock's face dropped.

"Impossible," Pinstripe growled. "No mortal can live that long and still look…"

Jennie shrugged. "As hot as me? I know. It's a good balance of diet, exercise, and… Oh, that's right. Kicking specter arse. Since I haven't done any of the latter yet today, would you two like to volunteer to be my first victims?"

Pinstripe growled, "Catch me if you can."

As he finished speaking, two things happened at once. The first was that Pinstripe chuckled and disappeared, leaving not even a drop of spectral energy in sight. The second was that Frock drew her own gun from behind her parasol and fired at Jennie.

Jennie ducked, having sensed that something like this would happen. "Nice try."

"I've got plenty more in the chamber." Frock grinned, sending off several more rounds.

Jennie dived out of the way and disappeared behind a dumpster as the bullets ricocheted around the alley. She knew she needed to drive the attack, but unfortunately, she'd learned she wasn't immune to either human or spectral bullets, a truth that was embossed on her body in the form of small balloon-knot scars on her arms, hips, and thighs.

Baxter had ducked back around the corner, and now sent off several shots of his own. His pistol fired true, but Frock managed to avoid each shot with a twirl of her parasol. She maneuvered as though dancing through the alley toward the fallen Tommy gun.

Jennie raised her pistol and shut one eye, aiming toward the Tommy gun to knock it farther away. Only, as she made to pull the trigger, she felt something hit her stomach *hard*.

She recovered from the sneak attack quickly, but more blows slammed into her. Each punch took the wind from her lungs and left marks on her skin.

Jennie tried to hit whatever was attacking her, but her hands passed through thin air.

"Oh, so you're one of *those*, are you? Well, it's been a while, but let's see if I can remember how to do this."

She ignored the assault, allowing the punches to force her against the wall. Before she knew it, she was sitting on her ass, blow after blow pounding into her cheeks as the fists connected and rattled her brain.

But her mind wasn't registering the physical pain she was in. She was deep inside her consciousness, hunting for the frequency at which Pinstripe was manifesting.

"Jennie?" Baxter called across the alley. "What are you doing?" When no answer came, he whispered to Worthington. "Is she okay?"

Worthington waved a hand. "Who knows? The woman is an enigma. Maybe focus on the girl about to pick up the Tommy gun instead."

"Right." Baxter glanced at Jennie uncertainly before firing several bullets at the ground around the gun.

One of the bullets slammed into Frock's hand and caused her to scream in pain. She shook it violently as though she had touched a scalding burner, and where her hand had been was now nothing more than a stump. She dropped her parasol with a glare at Baxter, dived to the ground, and picked up the gun.

Baxter burst around the corner and sprinted across the alley at an impressive speed. He jumped and landed on top of Frock as she was hunting for the trigger.

Given that the Tommy gun was a two-handed weapon, she was struggling even before the large, angry specter squished her.

Baxter grabbed Frock's functioning hand and pinned it to the ground, expecting her to yield the moment she realized she had been outmuscled.

Instead, Frock began trying to bite Baxter as though she was a hungry jackal.

Her teeth snapped near his ear as he moved away from her. "Yo, Worthington. If you could come over here and lend me a hand, that would be great."

But Worthington didn't know what to do. Between the invisible specter pummeling Jennie's face, and the rabid revolutionary wife gnashing at Baxter, the situation didn't look all that great.

"Hey! Mince-eater. Get your two-dollar ass over here before I make change!"

Worthington was shaken into action. He ran over to help Baxter, trying his best to keep his back straight so his hat didn't fall off his head.

Jennie saw none of this, however. She was deep inside her head, feeling the energies around her. She could vaguely make out the shapes of Worthington, Baxter, and Frock in her peripheral vision, but that wasn't where she was looking.

A shape that had been hidden in the energies surrounding her burned like volcanic fire. She could see Pinstripe as though she was looking through an infrared scope.

A small smirk appeared on her face, causing the invisible specter to hesitate.

Perfect.

It was all she needed. Now that she could see him, she could connect with him. She reached out to bind herself to him, and instantly felt the spectral energy flow within her. A moment later, her physical body disappeared from the alley as she plunged into the invisible sphere of the ethereal.

The world around her moved as if viewed from a car window speeding through a tunnel. The only clear thing before her was now Pinstripe, who stared at her in alarm.

"What are you?" he stuttered.

"Your worst nightmare," Jennie told him, punching him square in the nose. His nostrils exploded in a spray of spectral blood as the bridge was tweaked into a new position. She laughed. "Well, I never. Specters *can* bleed!"

Pinstripe shook his head and blocked the next punch. He ducked and aimed an uppercut at Jennie's midsection, but she was too quick.

She responded with a left hook and two right jabs that opened the split on his nose wider.

He stumbled back and tripped over his own feet.

Jennie took the opportunity. She straddled his body and returned the beating he'd given her minutes before. She laid into Pinstripe with blow after blow until he looked as if he was about to pass out.

"That'll do." She closed her eyes and converted his energy inside of her.

Meanwhile, Worthington and Baxter wrestled with Frock. She was surprisingly strong, given that she only had one functioning hand, but soon enough, they managed to get control of her.

Baxter held her arm pinned around her back while Worthington held the Tommy gun to her face, his hands shaking as his finger hovered over the trigger.

Frock grinned at Baxter. "You know if your friend shoots me with that, you're gonna catch the brunt of it?"

Baxter met Worthington's eyes. "If you so much as touch me with that thing, we're going to have a *big* problem," Baxter growled, causing Worthington to shake more. "You know, for one of the queen's guards, you're pretty uncertain when holding firearms."

"Just because I was charged with the protection of Elizabeth II in life and Queen Victoria in death, it doesn't mean I *like* to hurt people," he protested.

Baxter shrugged. "I'm just saying. It might be a useful skill to learn how to hold a gun without shaking in your boots, y'know?"

Worthington huffed and looked around the alley. "Where did Jennie go?"

They scanned the alley and could see no sign of either Jennie or Pinstripe. Even Frock craned her neck to get a better look, alarm spreading on her face.

"Is it possible that they both—" Worthington started, shutting off instantly when the figures of Jennie and Pinstripe reappeared suddenly in the alley.

She was still straddling him, one hand bunching up the material around his collar as the other hovered in a fist over his face.

"If you guys wanted some privacy, all you had to do was ask," Worthington called.

Jennie shook her head as if awaking from a dream. She looked down at Pinstripe. "Are you okay?"

He nodded, clearly confused by what had just happened.

"Good." Jennie punched him once more in the face, then got off him. She pulled him to his feet and marched him over to Frock. "Good work keeping that bitch down," she told Worthington and Baxter. "Now, if you two would be so kind as to tell us why you've been busy tagging the city, we can let you guys go and get on our merry way."

Pinstripe looked at Jennie with confusion. "Tagging?"

"Oh, sorry. I forgot you've been encased in rock for decades. Maybe 'tagging' is too contemporary for you. How about 'painting pictures on the fucking wall?'"

Pinstripe shook his head. "They made us. I swear to God, they made us."

Jennie looked at Baxter and Worthington, their eyes meeting hers with the same curious expression. "Who made you?"

"*They* did. The European ambassadors from the Winter Court," Frock replied. "They caught us after we were looking around the city for a safe place to go. Lured us in and made us take the sacred pledge to the queen. We had no choice. There were too many of them."

"Too many of *who*?" Jennie asked, growing frustrated.

"They wouldn't tell us their names, only that they had the power to exorcise us if we didn't comply. We were sent to recruit more specters and bring them to the crown on the orders of the queen. Being bound under our oath, what choice did we have?"

"I smell bullshit," Worthington mumbled without conviction.

Jennie ignored him. "These specters you speak of. There must be a hideout or somewhere they gather. You've been there, yes? You can tell us where they are."

Pinstripe shook his head. "Why would we tell you? We've sworn fealty to Her Majesty the Queen. To break the sacred oath would be treason, leading to our exorcisms. You think we'd do that to ourselves?" His head lowered. "I was just beginning to enjoy life in the modern world."

Frock nodded. "Me too."

"You've got it all wrong," Baxter told them, relaxing his grip on Frock slightly. "These two *are* from the Winter Court, aren't you? They've both taken the oath themselves, which means you're all on the same side, right?"

Worthington reluctantly nodded, clearly not happy to be associating himself as someone on the same side as these two.

Jennie remained quiet, her steely expression boring into the pair.

"Is this true?" Pinstripe asked. "You've sworn allegiance to the crown?"

Jennie didn't answer. Instead, she waited for Worthington, who stuck his pompous nose in the air as he spoke. "We have.

More than that, we report directly to Queen Victoria. Trusted advisors sent to this city to monitor the rising number of specters and ensuring that they serve the crown and commit to the queen's rules and laws."

"But we saw you with the enemy," Frock argued. "That night in Central Park? You were with them!"

"Who do you think set you two free?" Jennie held her gun in the air, showing them the weapon from which the bullet to distract Lupe and allow the specters to run away had been fired.

Pinstripe rose cautiously to his feet and brushed off his jacket. Already his nose was starting to move back into place, and the blood was drying up and disappearing. "So, we're really all on the same side?"

"It looks that way," Baxter told him.

Jennie held her gun for a moment longer before twirling it around her finger and replacing it in her holster. "At least for the time being. I would rather like to have a word with your superiors, though, and find out what the fuck the disconnect is in this city, and why they've sent two goons to bully a girl into joining the supernatural court." She turned to Worthington and raised a finger. "And before you open your mouth, something isn't right here, and you know it."

Worthington closed his mouth and cast his eyes to the ground.

CHAPTER NINETEEN

Brooklyn, New York City, Present Day

Jennie felt herself burning under the intensity of the cab driver's stare.

She was used to it by now. Sure, she knew her outfit was somewhat provocative to hot-blooded men with no more brain cells than a dung beetle, but that didn't mean she didn't get annoyed all the same.

It was a *fashion choice*. Not only did she want to look good while fighting, but the lack of bagginess also meant that enemies couldn't use her clothing to their advantage.

It also served a secondary purpose, too. Given that most of the scumbags she'd met in her life had been men leading organizations of men—even in the twenty-first century, how much of that had changed, really?—her little pieces of eye candy caused a great distraction to the guys who ogled her and underestimated her abilities when she went into action.

Who said a woman couldn't use her sexuality to her advantage?

But now, sitting in the back of the cab and watching the cab driver's eyes undress her, Jennie grew impatient. "Hey, eyes on the road, asshole," she snapped, distracting the driver from his reverie.

He clutched the steering wheel and jerked it to avoid drifting into the next lane.

"You'd think he'd take one look at the guns on your hips and think twice about mentally undressing you," Baxter remarked, sitting snuggly beside Jennie.

To his left, Frock—who she had since learned was named Rita—sat on Pinstripe—Rico's—lap, the two of them comically squashed against the window.

"Surely he's got more sense than that..." His voice trailed away as he looked at her hips and saw that her guns were gone.

Jennie smiled and snapped her fingers, and her guns reappeared as though they had been there all along.

Baxter gaped. "How did you..."

Jennie nodded at Worthington, who, unbeknownst to the driver, sat in the passenger seat. Only the bottom part of his hat could be seen since the rest of it now poked out of the roof of the car like some kind of fuzzy antennae.

"I can use my connection to Worthington to hide parts of me I don't want people to see," she replied quietly, aware that the cab driver was giving her a funny look again. She met his eye, and he looked sharply away. "It's part of my gift and something that helps me get around armed to the teeth in broad daylight. Back in the day, I used to be able to walk around with my pistols and no one would bat an eyelid. But now?" She sighed. "Now everything has changed."

"For the better, though, right?" Baxter asked.

Jennie didn't answer.

Rita leaned forward and pointed. The roads were quiet on this side of the Brooklyn Bridge, but now the taillights of the vehicles ahead blinked red as they approached a junction. "Take a left here."

Jennie repeated her instructions to the driver.

The pair navigated them deep into the heart of Brooklyn. They turned off the Fort Hamilton Parkway and pulled into Forty-Eighth Street.

The street was lined with suburban houses that had seen better days. Windows were cracked, and cars lined the streets. Several yards were bordered with mesh fences, and there was a smell of weed in the air.

"This is it?" Jennie asked, looking up and down the street.

"Not quite," Rico replied. "It's two blocks over, but we don't want to draw attention to it by parking directly outside. Particularly you, a strange human. This used to be a good neighborhood, but it's gone downhill in the last ten years. You'd get shot in a matter of seconds."

"That's something you don't hear every day," Jennie remarked. "The queen's people ready to blow out a stranger's brains on sight."

She thanked the driver and tossed him some cash, leaning through the gap between the seats so her breasts pushed out in front of her. He half-turned, eyebrows going up in surprise as he looked down at them.

"Hey, bozo, my eyes are up here." Jennie pulled her gun and pressed it into his side. "Just a word of advice. You're going to be a good little boy and keep your eyes and hands to yourself from now on. *Capiche?*"

The cabbie nodded emphatically.

Jennie lifted her gun and tapped the cab driver's cheek with the barrel. "Good. Because the last thing I'd want to do is hear a report on the radio about a sexy young woman gone missing and think you were somehow connected to it. That would be bad news for you, indeed."

The cab driver nodded his understanding and kept his eyes on the steering wheel as Jennie exited the cab. The moment the door closed behind her, he revved the engine and sped off into the night.

Baxter looked at her curiously. "What was that about?"

Jennie shrugged. "Oh, just a bit of housekeeping."

Rico and Rita took Jennie, Worthington, and Baxter around the corner to an empty, run-down house. Jennie drew from Worthington and turned herself spectral to make the shortcut easier to navigate. They passed through an overgrown yard, complete with a rusted and broken trampoline, and emerged onto Forty-Seventh Street, which was a mirror reflection of Forty-Eighth Street.

"They really need to invest some money in this neighborhood," Baxter commented. "There's so much money pumped into gambling, drinks, and narcotics, but these people have to live in poverty. It's just not right."

Jennie chuckled. "Well, maybe when the spectral world reveals itself to the mortals, you could run for councilor and make a difference."

Baxter shrugged at her dismissal. "You laugh, but I almost took a role in politics back in my day. Was going to put my name down to run for mayor until I discovered a passion for something else entirely."

"Gadgets?" Worthington inquired.

"Actually, no. That came later. It was my first wife." He looked at the stars, eyes growing foggy with memory. "Ah, Christine. You were the only woman I ever loved."

"Aw, what happened?" Rita asked. "Lose her when you died?"

"Unfortunately, no," Baxter replied, suddenly looking embarrassed. "Truth was that she didn't understand my passion for inventing, so she left me for the neighbor's brother. Last I heard, they went to the West Coast and I haven't heard from them since."

"That's a shame," Rita sympathized. "Everyone deserves to be in love."

"Oh, I loved." Baxter grinned. "I loved with everything I had. I sometimes think I used all my love with Christine on a fire that burned so intensely that I had nothing left to give after a time."

"How long were you together?" she asked.

"Eight months," Baxter replied simply.

Rita stared at him with an open mouth as he passed her.

Jennie caught up with Rico as they passed through another house. This house was in a much better state than the previous one, although it was without many of the luxuries people found affordable. The floor was stained and filthy, and somewhere upstairs, someone snored.

Jennie shook her head, unable to believe people lived like this.

"That's not a long time," Pinstripe muttered.

Baxter shrugged. "I guess. It was enough."

Rita sighed. "I wish I could still see my lover. Donavon Mayhew. He was a dreamboat."

"What happened to him?" Baxter asked.

"It was more like what happened to *me*," Rita replied. "On the day he set out to join the Revolution, I couldn't let him go. I don't know what came over me, but I trailed him and his cohort of soldiers too close to the battlefield. I loved him. That love was all-consuming, and I needed to know he was okay.

"What I didn't know was that the enemy had set up an ambush. A small group of their main force peeled off and snuck behind our lines." Her eyes narrowed. "I saw one of them pull out his rifle from a nearby bush, and I screamed like I'd never screamed before. Turns out they were ready to silence anyone who got in their way."

She placed a hand over the bullet wound on her chest and gave a nostalgic smile. "It should've hurt, but I think I was dead before the pain registered."

They made it to the back of the house, where Rico paused and placed an ear against the wall.

Jennie was enraptured by Rita's story. She wanted to find out more. There was one part she didn't understand. "So, how did you find yourself encased in a boulder?" she asked, ignoring the surprised look from Baxter, who was hearing this for the first time. "Once a person dies, their spirit is set free. I've never heard of or seen what happened to you before."

Rita's face grew dark. "Donavon tried to save my body and bring me back to life. There was a rumor that a gaggle of witches still remained from the end of the Salem trials some hundred years previous. I don't know how he found them, and I can't say for sure that they were witches, but whoever they were, there was dark magic there. They did something that sank my physical and spiritual body into that boulder and wouldn't let me go."

"A similar thing happened to me," Rico told them. "They said it was for my own good. That placing me inside the boulder would bring me immortality. That when I finally did break free, the world would be at peace, and I would unite with my mortal body and live forever." He snorted. "Can't believe I thought that might actually happen."

"Why would you want to return to a mortal body when you can live as a specter?" Baxter asked. "I've never been happier than I am now."

Rita and Rico looked at each other sadly. Rico sighed. "Because you can always guarantee you've got at least one extra shot at life."

Rico said no more on the matter, and Jennie and the others didn't feel the need to press him.

Worthington folded his arms and tapped his feet. "Are we finished with storytime? Because I thought we were here to achieve something tonight."

Rico grinned, the sight of it rather wolfish. "Right you are, Beefeater."

"It's…" Worthington smiled. "Oh, thank you."

Rico nodded at Rita, and they slipped through the wall and out of sight.

"They're a strange pair," Baxter commented.

Worthington walked off. "I like them."

"Only because they finally got your job title right." Jennie chuckled before following him outside. Baxter came shortly after.

As Jennie materialized through the wall, she knew that something was wrong. The first sign was that Rita and Rico stood facing them in the middle of the road. The second was that Worthington wriggled between them, caught in their grip. The third was that their weapons were trained on his heart and head.

And the final thing? Well, that was the handful of armed thugs leaning out of the abandoned building's second-floor windows, their guns trained on Jennie and Baxter.

The hairs on the back of Jennie's neck stood on end. "How many times do I have to tell you, Jennie?" She mumbled to herself. "Specters *cannot* be trusted."

"Hey!" Baxter's complaint turned into a gulp when Rico began to laugh.

CHAPTER TWENTY

<u>**Loew's Forty-Sixth Street Theater, Brooklyn, Present Day**</u>

Vinnie Romano looked down his nose at the poor excuses for specters sitting in the theater's dressing rooms.

Bulbs still bordered the mirrors, although the glass of each was either smashed or thick with dust. Stools had been knocked over and were so rusted they were orange, and what had once been plush leather sofas for the celebrities who'd graced these walkways were nothing more than chewed up piss-stained couches with their springs sticking out like insect appendages.

Three specters sat on the floor, slumped against the walls. Vinnie had seen their type before. Three former crack addicts who were only now just beginning to get their heads around the fact that they would never feel the highs of narcotics again.

The floor was littered with needles they couldn't touch, the syringes lined with the remnants of the final fix that had caused them to breathe their last breath and enter the world beyond life.

They scratched their arms and they shivered where they sat, and their spectral skin was covered in sores.

Vinnie wrinkled his nose, knowing that the other dressing rooms held similar scenarios. A plethora of the city's lowest of the low, coming to terms with their new existence as the world swam beneath their feet.

"It gets easier," he told them without compassion.

They didn't even look at him, merely grunted. He hated that he had to associate with these degenerates.

Vinnie weighed the pistol in his hand and fought the desire to use it on them. As satisfying as it would be, it was hardly relevant to his purpose. They needed all the help they could get, no matter where they got it from.

He closed the door on them and wandered down the corridors.

The old theater was a mess, having closed to the public over fifty years ago. The city of New York hadn't bothered to renovate the damned thing, just left it to rot. The walls were mostly bare wood, with yellowed wallpaper peeling from the tops like curled fingernails. The lights and abandoned furniture were caked in dust.

The corners of this place were a hungry spider's wet dream.

It was the perfect place for a hideout, somewhere considered haunted by the locals and forgotten by the politicians. A piece of history standing on a cliff face, bravely rooting itself in the face of a storm.

Vinnie passed several other cruel-faced specters but uttered no greeting. Over his years of death, he had learned when to speak and when to remain silent. Even now, as several other specters ran toward the upper windows and withdrew their weapons, he refused to open his mouth.

He rounded the corner and walked the stairs leading to the theater's upper balcony. He emerged into the old auditorium and looked out on the rows of faded red seating facing a stage that would never be used again. That was the thing about death; you learned what it was to be useless and lonely.

A single specter sat in the center row, arms spread out and relaxed over the backs of the adjacent chairs.

"Nearly showtime," the specter called, his voice echoing around the hall. "Nearly fifty years on, and we're finally about to watch what we've all been waiting for."

Vinnie walked down the row and took a seat behind the specter. "Ain't you needed upstairs?"

"Nah." The specter grinned. "This is where it's all going to take place. Down on that stage, where the magic is supposed to happen. You ever seen a stage show, Vinnie?"

Vinnie only shook his head, but somehow, the specter knew what he was saying.

"They're a marvel. Lights, actors, dancers—oh, man, you should see the dancers. Leggy blondes who could kick the faces off the VIPs in the wings."

"I don't see any dancers," Vinnie told him.

"Observant, ain't ya?" The specter pulled out a ghostly cigar from his pocket. "No, you're right. No dancers today, Vinnie. No dancers, but there will be a show, that's for sure. There's always a show whenever she's around."

Vinnie gulped. He knew who the specter was talking about, of course. He had encountered her before, a long time ago, a brief encounter that had ended in his and many of his comrades' deaths.

"We can beat her, can't we?" Vinnie asked, a fragment of doubt in his voice.

Marco turned in his seat, his hardened stare drilling into Vinnie from beneath his brow. Half of his cheek was missing, and there was a large hole in his stomach from where the Big Bitch had shot him.

Marco moved so suddenly that Vinnie barely had a chance to retaliate. He grabbed Vinnie by the ear and pulled him so close that their noses were virtually touching.

"Yeah, we can," Marco growled. "Because if we fail this time, we're both out of chances. No more resurrection as spectral entities, no. If we die now, we're dead forever. You hear me?"

Vinnie swallowed and raised an eyebrow. "I didn't think she could exorcise specters?"

Marco gave an infinitesimal shake of his head. "It doesn't matter. If we don't finish her off this time, then she's not the one we need to worry about, is she?"

Marco threw Vinnie back against the seat where he shrunk and passed through the ancient fabric. A gun fired somewhere outside, and both of their eyes moved to the exit doors at the back of the theater.

Marco gave a wicked grin. "Oh, good, the curtains are up. Time to get this show rolling."

"I do have to warn you that there is only one way that this will end if you choose to get on my bad side." Jennie held up her hands as though she were being placed under arrest, yet her expression was calm and collected. "Is that what you want to do?"

Rico turned to the gunmen on the upper levels and laughed once more. "She's kidding, right? You do know you're outnumbered and that we have your spectral buddy hostage?"

"I told you they weren't working for the crown," Worthington cried, struggling to escape as he was dragged away. "I fucking *told* you."

Rita tightened her grip around his arm and dug her pistol into his stomach. "Oh, no. That part was all true. We're all working for the same mistress, only you two have stumbled upon something Her Majesty would rather not have made public."

A flicker of doubt passed across Jennie's face. Her eyes met Worthington's, and he looked away.

Jennie controlled her emotions, ensuring that her enemy couldn't see what was going on in her head. The strongest weapon any person—alive or dead—could harness, was their confidence. The moment that slipped, the floodgates would open, and the enemy would tear into it and use it to their advantage.

"What is it you want?" Jennie asked. "Clearly there's some kind of motive here, so what is it? What do you want from us?"

Rico sneered. "It's not what *I* want. It's more what my superiors want. Come along quietly, and perhaps we'll give you an honorable entry into death. Do you know the suffering that can be inflicted before a person dies?" He shook his head and tutted. "It's beyond description."

Jennie turned to Baxter, whose eyes were fixed on the thugs up above them.

The only redeeming factor of this building was a small section cut into the corner, which had since been converted into Regal's Fine Furniture store, a small shop that made use of the theater's old reception area.

The rest of the building looked like it had lain untouched for decades.

"What do you think, big guy?" Jennie asked Baxter out of the corner of her mouth. "Do we surrender?"

"I didn't have you down as the surrendering type," he implied.

Jennie contemplated that. "You know, you're right. But it's been a while since I've seen a theater from the fifties, and I'm itching to get inside."

Baxter finally tore his eyes away from the gunmen and looked at Jennie. To another person he might have been intimidating, looming almost two feet taller than Jennie.

However, she had seen bigger and badder in her days.

Baxter grinned. "There's more than one way to break into a theater."

Jennie nodded. "Good answer."

A second later, Jennie's pistol was in her hand. She took aim at the windows and took out one of the gunmen in a single shot. Then she connected with Baxter, and they both became immaterial and melted through the wall of the house behind them.

CHAPTER TWENTY-ONE

A volley of glowing bullets ricocheted off the back of the house, raining spectral dust to the ground.

Jennie heard them all, as loud as hands clapping, but she knew the residents of the house wouldn't. Mortals were unable to hear virtually *anything* that happened outside of their range of frequency, and it was only a few conduits and gifted among them who were able to experience the sounds and cries of the dead.

Jennie had experienced this all of her life, from spectral children playing outside at night to former lovers meeting in the afterlife and throwing themselves into cries of passion. From gang members still wrapped up in their feuds to former opera singers unable to let their music go. She could hear it all.

Her parents never could. Nor could any of her friends—when she'd still bothered with the living, that was.

During these times, she had merely clutched her hands to her head, praying for the voices to stop. The other children would ask her what was wrong, but she had learned over time to avoid telling them the truth, just drew herself into a tight bubble of reclusion.

It was only after the battle for the paranormal courts at the start of the twentieth century when Victoria took her place as queen and Jennie was fully indoctrinated into the paranormal world that she began to understand the limits of mortals, and the extent of her own powers.

Oh, yes. They slept silently, waking in the morning none the wiser to the events that would take place at night and the ground-shaking shift of faith that would tear the paranormal court wide open.

Baxter held his pistol near his face, his back to the wall. "Is your friend going to be okay out there?"

Jennie winked. "*My* friend? I thought he was yours."

Baxter laughed. "Seriously."

"He'll be fine," Jennie assured him. "He's hardly going to be in much danger out there. What's the worst they can do to him? Blow off his face and shut him up for a few seconds?"

"They could exorcize him," Baxter suggested.

"True." Jennie dismissed the thought. "But they'd need someone extra-powerful for that kind of ritual. Given that they're just a bunch of mobsters holed up in an old theater, I'm going to assume he'll be just fine on his own."

More shots rang out.

"Time to get out of here." Jennie crossed the living room and opened the door to the kitchen. She paused when she saw a boy of around six years of age standing in the milky light of the refrigerator with a carton of orange juice in his hand.

Jennie froze.

The boy turned and stared at her with wide eyes. The orange juice fell from his hands.

"You can see me?" she asked softly.

The boy nodded his head.

Shit, she thought. *Always check that you're in spectral form before running uninvited through someone else's house.*

She waved her hands in front of her as if casting a spell. "This is *all* a dream…"

The next moment she reconnected to Baxter and disappeared from sight. She left the boy standing there with the pool of orange juice dampening his socks. A second later, she had passed through the wall to the front of the building and found somewhere new to hide.

For the first time in decades, Worthington felt the pain of being beaten.

They had not been gentle with him. Rico and Rita had dragged him through the theater walls and past the gunmen lining the corridors inside.

There were a couple hundred of them, at least—specters with scars on their skin and permanent scowls on their faces. The theater smelled of death and an abandonment of hope. They passed rooms lined with specters overcoming withdrawal, and others containing prostitutes who now satisfied the dead instead of the living.

Several rooms they passed were used as weapons stores. The specters who had died with their guns in their hands had donated their ghostly firearms to the cause.

The place was huge. They went up flight after flight of stairs until they reached the VIP lounge—a large room complete at the very top of the building with a bar and several pool tables. One of the tables sported a broken leg that made it bow crookedly to the others.

"You're going to regret treating me this way," Worthington told them through gritted teeth.

Rico raised the back of his hand as if intending to slap Worthington. He flinched and closed his eyes, thankful when someone shouted, "Stop," and the pain he had expected didn't come.

Worthington opened his eyes and saw two specters sitting in

armchairs in the lounge. They both wore suits that had permanent bloodstains on their shirts. The one on the left looked fairly whole, whereas the one on the right had a large chunk missing from his right cheek.

"Welcome!" The one on the right spread his arms wide as he spoke as if he was greeting an old friend. "Who do we have here?"

Worthington tugged his arms out of Rico and Rita's grasp and dusted off his clothes. He adjusted his bearskin hat to try to recover a modicum of self-respect. "Worthington Conrad, Beefeater and subject of Queen Victoria. Sent on an errand to this country to—"

"Hush, hush," the specter interrupted Worthington, puffing on his cigar. Ghostly smoke curled out of his mouth, leaking through the hole in his cheek like water through a burst pipe. "I asked you a simple question, and I now have my answer. Learn when to shut up."

"You sound just like Jennie," Worthington mumbled.

The specter continued as if Worthington hadn't spoken. "Pleased to meet you, Worthington. My name's Marco Ruggiero, and this here is my associate, Vinnie Romano. We understand you've been causing my men some trouble?"

"I know who you are," Worthington replied, his face turning dark. "The queen warned me that I might run into you two. Tell me, how go the recruiting efforts in the city? Because you're doing a bang-up job of keeping quiet and avoiding stirring up trouble."

A flutter of annoyance crossed Marco's features at Worthington's sarcastic reply.

Vinnie gave a cursory glance his way. "So, it's true. You *are* here on the queen's business. What right does the queen have to meddle in our efforts? The last we heard, we're supposed to grow her numbers of followers in the US. Find new recruits and squash any competition."

"If that's the case, you're doing a shit job," Worthington said.

Rico and Rita shuffled awkwardly beside him, unsure of what was going on or what to say. "The Spectral Plane has made enough of a stir that they've been noticed in Britain. You think the queen didn't hear of the battle you fought several months ago? How long did you think you could keep that one quiet?"

Marco's brow furrowed, and he stared angrily at Worthington. "What does Her Majesty want with us? We're doing her bidding. We're keeping our end of the bargain."

Worthington gave them a hard look. "If that were true, why would she send Rogue across the Atlantic to clean up your mess?"

At the sound of Jennie's name, what little color remained in Vinnie's face drained. His hands moved down from his chest to cover the hole she had left in his stomach.

"What's your part in all this?" Marco growled, his anger finally making its way to the surface. "Surely Rogue doesn't need a babysitter. Why have you been sent here?"

"To keep the bitch off your trail and take down the Spectral Plane," Worthington replied.

Marco grinned. "Well, if that's the case, then *you've* done a shitty job."

"I did what I could." Worthington scowled. "It's not my fault you left a trail of breadcrumbs leading directly to your fucking front door."

"No, but since she's your charge, it's you who assumes responsibility." Marco continued to grin. "Queeny won't be too happy to learn you failed in your mission, will she?"

At this, a corresponding grin grew on Worthington's face. "She doesn't have to find out. Guess who's got a plan to ensure that she gets captured and removed from the equation?"

Vinnie leaned forward in his chair. "How? *How?*"

Worthington chuckled darkly. "Because the bitch is mortal, and if there's one thing mortals do a thousand times better than us specters, it's dying."

Jennie peered out from around the side of the pillar.

She had snuck through the houses, courtesy of Baxter's power. They had moved fast and been able to shake off the dozens of specters that had spilled from the theater and stationed themselves around the block to act as sentries against the mortal who was able to harness the powers of the ethereal.

A train passed overhead. The concrete pillars supporting the track were broad, and strong enough to support the weight while preventing any specters from being able to see her.

"There'll be a back entrance," Baxter told Jennie. "A door used by the A-listers and the techies. If we can make it there, we should be set."

"You think they won't guard the back door?" Jennie asked incredulously.

"You think they will?" Baxter replied

"Of course," Jennie assured him. "This isn't my first rodeo. Expect everywhere to be covered, and you'll never be taken by surprise."

"Then how are we going to get in?" His eyes lit up. "Are you going invisible again?"

Jennie shook her head, not taking her eyes off the gunmen stalking the street ahead. "I realize there's no way you'd know this, but that's not how my powers work."

"How *do* they work?" Baxter inquired.

Jennie put her hands on her hips. "Do you really expect me to waste time talking you through my process when we've got a band of gunmen looking for us, *and* they have taken my specter hostage?"

Baxter stared at her expectantly.

Jennie rolled her eyes. "Fine. Here's the short version: in order for my powers to work, I have to be within a certain range of another specter. Ordinarily, I'm bound to powers based on the type of specter—DNA, bloodline, where they're from and such—but sometimes, depending on the energy of a specter, I can harness powers beyond my usual range. That trick you saw with Rico and me becoming invisible? I was only able to harness that because he owned that power. That wasn't something I could do with everyone, as useful as it would be."

"So, your powers," Baxter pressed. "They're dependent on the powers the specter possesses?"

"Most of the time." Jennie ducked behind the pillar as a gunman looked their way. "Sometimes a specter has a special reserve of energy I can tap into and perform certain miracles. I don't always know what will happen, but over the years, I've learned to predict the outcome of a sudden burst of spectral energy."

Baxter looked at Jennie with awe. "Fascinating."

"Don't look at me like that."

"Like what?" Baxter asked.

"Like you want to dissect me and study my components," Jennie told him. "I'm not an iPhone you can take apart and reverse-engineer."

Baxter blew out a puff of air. "Don't even get me started on those things. The days I spent watching over the shoulders of the technicians in the phone repair shops, and I still don't understand it. To fit that amount of gadgetry to power into such a small processor..."

"*Now.*"

Baxter broke out of his mental image of the internal components of the iPhone as Jennie sprinted across the road and toward the next pillar. He glanced at the street and saw that his chance was still open, so sped to catch up with her.

They skirted the front face of the theater, passing the furniture store under the cover of darkness. Occasionally they had to stop and wait for a gunman to go by before they eventually made it to the street across from the back door.

To Jennie's dismay, a rotund gentleman specter in a suit and red tie stood in front of the back door with an AK-47 in his hands.

Jennie's eyes lit up. "That's a big baby."

Baxter snickered. "Aren't we all technically 'big babies?'"

Jennie shot Baxter a look. "You know the last specter I had who couldn't keep his mouth shut got taken captive by a spectral mob, right? Learn from his mistakes and keep quiet. I don't actually need you to break inside."

"Wrong," Baxter winked. "You said it yourself; you need a specter nearby to activate your powers." He spread his arms wide, presenting himself like a trophy. "Well, here I am."

Whatever Baxter had expected as a response, it wasn't what happened. He had thought Jennie would surrender; admit that she needed him and begin to draw power off him. Instead, she broke free of their cover and sprinted into the open.

Baxter's mouth dropped open. "What are you…"

The rotund specter's eyes widened with alarm. He aimed the spectral AK-47 at Jennie and made to shoot.

She ran across the street, closing the gap in seconds as she focused her energy. She connected to the specter before his trigger finger could pull and tore the gun from his grip.

She turned the barrel toward the specter.

His mouth dropped open and he muttered several incomprehensible words before the butt of the assault rifle smacked him in the face.

He fell and covered his head with his arms as he quivered on the floor.

Jennie turned the barrel back toward his head and growled at him as Baxter caught up with them both.

"How many of them are behind the door?" Jennie barked.

The man stuttered, his eyes screwed shut.

"How many!" She poked the barrel at his nose, causing him to open his eyes and yelp in alarm.

"I...I d-don't know," he stammered. "I was told to cover the back entrance. That was the only instruction I had, I swear."

Baxter looked at the pitiful man. "Not the toughest nut to crack, was he?"

Jennie shrugged. "That's what happens when you force recruits to join your cause. You don't get the best, you just bolster your numbers and fill your clubhouse with imbeciles."

She reached down and dragged the man to his feet before wrapping an arm around his throat and holding him in front of her.

She tossed the AK-47 to Baxter. "Here. This is yours now." She marched forward and disappeared through the door.

Baxter rolled the rifle over in his hands, examining it as though Jennie had just tossed him something covered in dog shit. "If it's okay with you, I'll stick to my good ol' reliable," he told Jennie, following her into the building.

CHAPTER TWENTY-TWO

They emerged into a wide corridor that led to the staging area. Faded posters lined the walls, with instructions for the crew and the acts about how to access the dressing rooms and some house-keeping rules.

Jennie felt that familiar buzz of excitement as she tiptoed ahead, the same buzz she felt every time she entered a theater—as though anything was possible, and the imagination was just the doorway to a better reality.

Posters were crookedly displayed in frames. One poster showed seventies hippie types flowing around an illustration of a band Jennie hadn't heard in years. The words, "Jefferson Airplane" in bold, with additional text beneath yielding the dates to their 1970 tour.

There were posters for The Grateful Dead, and The Byrds, to name but a few. The final remnants of the last acts to ever play in the theater before its closure. A time when the auditorium was filled with the cheers of the crowd and the harmonic blaring of bands who would be all but lost to memory.

Jennie veered to her left, toward a door with a star on the

outside. Whoever's name had been last imprinted on the star was now nothing more than a black smudge.

She shoved the specter out in front of her with the Big Bitch wedged between his shoulder blades and nudged the door open to peek inside.

"What are you doing?" Baxter hissed.

Jennie ignored him. While she was here, she figured she'd at least take a look around. Why not soak in a bit of historical culture in the middle of a gang raid in which all members were focused on hunting her down?

The door creaked open, and Jennie could only stare. Slumped against the wall were several specters, their bodies gaunt and thin, their arms pocked with marks. The instruments they used for self-medication littered the floor around them.

A wave of nausea washed over her. She had never seen anything like this. During her time exploring the world of the dead, she had seen a great many sights, but nothing quite as disturbing as this.

"Didn't mean to bother you," she whispered to the room before backing out.

There was no reply.

"What the hell are these people thinking?" Jennie whispered, looking back down the corridor and eyeing the other dressing rooms.

Were they all full of deceased drug addicts?

Muffled grunts and moans told her that probably wasn't the case.

"I don't know," Baxter answered. He held his wrench tightly in one hand, while his pistol was gripped in the other. The wrench hung by his side, making his already gorilla-like arms look longer and more formidable than before. "But I don't really want to find out."

Jennie internally agreed but remained silent. She made her

way to the end of the corridor and paused to place her ear against the door.

She could hear voices on the other side—hushed murmurs from the enemy. She closed her eyes and tried to understand what they were saying.

"Gone, just like that," a female voice hissed. "Just like one of us."

"That's impossible," another replied. "No mortal can vanish like that."

A third voice spoke up. "What about those people with gifts? You know…oh, what are they called? Candidates?"

"*Conduits*, idiot," the second voice corrected. "And no. Even conduits can't just disappear. They can hear and see us, but they can't just vanish."

"We'll find them soon. We always do," the first voice asserted. "I don't care what the bosses say about her, she's no match for our weapons. If she can become a specter, then she can be harmed like a specter."

"Haven't you heard the stories?" the third voice asked uncertainly. "She's not just a mortal or a specter. They say she's called 'Rogue.' I heard she once went through an entire house full of mortals and killed everyone before they even had a chance to raise the alarm."

"Where did you hear that?" The first voice sounded skeptical, a note of laughter in her words. "No mortal has that amount of skill."

The third voice spoke up again. "It's how the bosses died. I overheard them speaking last night. She shot them at point-blank range. They didn't stand a chance."

The second person blew a raspberry. "Oh, behave. That was when they were mortal. Mortals are notoriously easy to kill. Let's just see how she deals with taking down a bunch of specters. I'm sure that'll put a hole in her tires—"

Jennie chose that moment to appear through the door. The three specters were gathered at the foot of a staircase. One of them sat on the bottom step, while another leaned on the handrail. The third rested his back against the wall, pistol dangling lazily by his side.

"I can give you a demonstration if you'd like?" Jennie offered, enjoying the sudden scramble as the three rushed to raise their guns and aim them at her.

Jennie's hostage began thrashing again, fear taking over as he fought to release himself from her grip.

Jennie tightened her hold on him and aimed the Big Bitch at his temple.

"You shoot me, I shoot him. Does that work for everybody?"

The three specters hesitated for only a moment before firing their guns.

The reports were deafening. The rotund specter grunted and spluttered as bullets tore into him, the spectral metal piercing his large stomach. He tried to call out to the others to ask them to stop but couldn't get a word out as his body was pricked like a pin cushion.

At least they will have gotten her, too, he thought with an odd sense of satisfaction. If the bullets had gone through him, chances were they would have penetrated the woman behind him, too.

After several seconds, they stopped firing. The rotund specter smiled and fell to his knees, words forming on his lips but no sound coming out.

The three specters' faces fell when they saw that there was no girl behind their comrade—not even the ghost of the girl they had just battered with bullets.

The woman looked for Jennie in shock. "What the fuck?"

"Where'd she go?" the second asked.

Suddenly the rotund man let out a gasp. "My leg," he cried. "She's pulling my leg."

They craned their heads enough to see Jennie's spectral hand clamped to the specter's ankle.

They heard her laughter coming from somewhere beneath them.

Jennie took advantage of her immaterial state and swung from his leg and through the concrete below like a spectral Tarzan. She released her grip at the right moment on the upswing to land in front of them and fire the Big Bitch into the face of the woman.

Her head exploded into pieces, leaving nothing behind but the ghostly stump of her neck.

"Aw, now is definitely a bad time to lose your head," she crooned, immediately holstering the Big Bitch and grabbing the second specter by the neck.

Foregoing his weapon, he tried to claw Jennie's face, hoping to find some way to get purchase and break her grip. Unfortunately, all he succeeded in doing was giving her the momentum to take a small jump from the stairs and slam him into the ground.

The specter cried out and massaged his neck, leaving Jennie enough time to take out number three.

Or so she thought.

As she spun around, she found herself looking directly down the barrel of a pistol.

The sound of running feet was all around them now as the alarm was raised and specters began flooding back into the theatre to help out.

The specter holding the pistol smirked. "Oh, I so wanted to be the one to capture you," he told Jennie with a stupid grin on his face.

He thumbed off the safety. "Now, would you please follow me—"

Jennie caught a flash of metal followed by a heavy crunching sound as Baxter swung his wrench in a deadly arc and drove it into the specter's skull, causing his head to dent into the shape of a heart.

"You can't say the kid doesn't have manners," he commented, breathing heavily. He looked at the other two specters. "You really don't pull your punches, do you?"

"Not when I have cause to," she replied, keeping her eyes on Baxter as she drew her pistol and shot to the side. A grunt followed as the rotund specter who had been crawling to pick up his comrade's weapon yowled in pain.

Shouts rang from all around. Figures appeared at the top of the stairs. Bullets rained down upon them. Jennie grabbed Baxter's arm and dragged him out of range, moving away from the stairs and through a door to the side.

Several more armed specters were there to greet them, the surprise on their faces quickly replaced by the excitement of catching the enemy.

Jennie pulled Baxter back, and they sprinted past the stairs again. A bullet whizzed by her ear, close enough that she could hear the whistle. She found another door and was met by more armed specters. Another turn, another door, and even more appeared. Soon enough, every exit was blocked.

"Well, we had a good run," Baxter told Jennie. "At least we tried, eh?"

Jennie placed her hands in the air, then laced her fingers behind her head and got to her knees.

"What are you doing?" Baxter asked.

She shrugged. "Cooperating."

Baxter hesitated, then, seeing the number of guns aimed at him, he fell to his knees, too. "Okay. It's just, I've never seen you cooperate before."

"What can I say? I'm full of surprises."

Apparently, so are these guys, Jennie thought as footsteps on the stairs signaled the arrival of two men. She recognized them but couldn't place where she knew them from.

CHAPTER TWENTY-THREE

The leader of the pack, a man who looked like a large portion of his genetic code was Italian and who had an accent to match, snapped his fingers and sneered. Specters tied blindfolds around Jennie's and Baxter's heads before they marched them through the theater toward an unknown destination.

After a surprisingly short amount of time, Jennie was shoved to her knees again and the hands released her, leaving her and Baxter in a silence that was altogether unsettling.

"You should know I don't do so well with quiet," Jennie called to people she wasn't even sure were there. "That's why I shoot so much. Guns speak rather loudly. They silence the neuroses arguing in my head and ensure that I don't go crazy."

"We're all crazy here," a voice growled from somewhere far away. "That's the beauty of it all. The crazy ones should stick together, no? Otherwise, how will we survive in this increasingly crazy world?"

Jennie tensed. She knew that voice. Knew it rather well, but hadn't heard it in...years? Decades?

"Crazy is beautiful, for the most part," Jennie called back. "Except when it comes from the psychos. The murderers, the rapists, the addicts. Then crazy can become a dangerous thing. I should know, I've snuffed out enough of the crazies to save the mortals that I'm something of an expert on it."

A pause.

"Hello?"

Silence.

"You know it's rude to ignore people?"

A second voice spoke. She could practically hear the smile on his face. "Crazy is as crazy does. It's just a shame you won't be able to save the dead the way that you saved the mortals all those years ago."

There was the sound of a struggle, and a man cried out muffled words.

A moment later, Jennie heard Worthington's sobs. "Please, Jennie! Do as they say. They'll let us go. Just listen to their demands, and we can go back to England. They've promised us life if we turn back now."

Jennie bit her lip, her frustration growing as the identity of the speakers continued to evade her. She could see their shapes in her head as nothing more than silhouettes.

"Oh, Worthington, you know I can't do that," Jennie replied placidly. "See, the problem with me is that once I get a whiff of injustice, I can't be shaken off the scent—particularly by those who tarnish the queen's honor and try to run their own regime in her name. So, what'll it be, dirtbags? Are you going to come willingly, or do I have to make a ruckus and fuck your shit up?"

A moment later, she heard the dirty chuckles. They were raspy, the sounds of a chain smoker who had made it into their fifties and now lived with a permanent frog in their throat. "Oh, Rogue. You haven't changed a bit, have you?"

"Why would I change?" she replied. "I was born perfect. I'm sure I'll die that way."

"Oh, we'll make sure of that," the second voice told her. "Although you haven't changed much, I think it's safe to say that we have." Another cocky chuckle. "This time, you can't harm us. This time, we are truly *bulletproof*."

Blinding light attacked Jennie's eyes as the blindfolds were ripped away from her and Baxter's heads. Now she knew who was running the show—the Messino brothers.

Jennie and Baxter knelt in the center of the stage in a harsh cone of light cast by spotlights. Jennie shaded her eyes with a hand and saw the outline of the Messino brothers sitting on the front row of the upper balcony. One of them was leaning over the railing, and the other sat back in his chair with his legs crossed and a smile on his face.

Gathered behind Jennie and Baxter in a semi-circle were two dozen specters, each with their weapon trained on Jennie and Baxter. Among the lineup, she spotted Rico, Rita and...

Charles?

Her mind connected the dots.

Revolter. It all makes sense now.

Worthington stood just off the stage, held at gunpoint by two men in suits with severe gunshot wounds.

Baxter grumbled, his head turning as he counted all the guns targeting him and Jennie. "Ah, man, this is going to hurt."

Jennie, meanwhile, simply stared at the balcony with a smile on her face. "Eugenio. Carmelo. How long has it been?"

"Too long," Eugenio told her, rising from his seat and making his way down the stairs toward the stage. "You know, I have to thank you, Rogue. You did us a favor all those years ago. I couldn't see it at the time, but the years passed, and old wounds healed. Now we've got much more to be grateful for."

Carmelo followed his brother down the stairs, still clearly the quieter of the two.

"Oh? What's that?" Jennie asked as several more specters appeared from the doors to the wings and the lobby. "You've finally learned not to kidnap young girls from their families where they'll be abused all their life? I see you've upgraded to using the unfortunates to get your way. Where are you keeping the pimps?"

Eugenio reached the front row and took a seat in the center. His brother joined him shortly after. "Oh, no. No pimps. Just hos. Addicts. Convicts. Those who the city failed to help, and who deserve another chance in the afterlife. I like to think of it as an afterlife rehabilitation program in the name of Queen Victoria."

Jennie cocked her head. "I keep hearing Her Majesty's name thrown around in this city, but there's one thing I can't work out."

"What's that?" Eugenio asked.

"Why?" Jennie replied. "If Queen Victoria sent me to deal with the rising number of non-aligned specters, why would she bother dealing with dirtbags like you?"

Eugenio grinned and turned to his brother.

Carmelo finally spoke up. "It's a pretty sweet deal, actually. Did you know that Queen Victoria is the longest-serving paranormal monarch ever to have existed? Yeah, it's true."

Jennie rolled her eyes. "A history lesson from a kid. Perfect." She sighed. "Very well, continue."

"Have you never wondered why that is?" He began to count on his fingers. "George II took the paranormal throne from 1760–1820. He held it for sixty years, until George III died and inherited it.

"George III held it from 1820–1830. That's ten years. George IV held it from 1830–1837. That's seven years. William IV held it from 1837–1901. That's sixty-four years, the longest any paranormal king or queen has held the throne."

"Until Victoria," Eugenio cut in as though this whole thing had been rehearsed. "In life, she held the record for the longest-running British monarch of her time. Quite a feat, really. Over half a century of ruling the British people."

Carmelo lowered his hands, a mocking grin on his face. "But she had one fatal flaw, didn't she? In extending her rule, she lessened that of her successor. Edward VII died just nine years later, giving Queen Victoria only nine years to rule as queen of the Winter Court." He shook his head. "Such a sad, sad thing."

"So, what to do when her eldest remaining heir dies and appears at her door in the Winter Court? Nine years is a short time to rule in the afterlife when you were the longest ruler of the British Empire in life."

Jennie remained silent, her lips tightening. She felt a wave of anger roiling deep inside her but knew she needed to hear the rest of the tale. She had always wondered how the line of succession worked for the court. She had even asked a few people in her time, but had been met with silence and fear.

Baxter growled, following their train of thought. "She hires men like you."

Carmelo turned to Baxter, impressed. "Well done, Brutus." He chuckled.

Eugenio kept his attention on Jennie. "Did you really think we had no motive for doing the things we did in life? Your queeny made a deal with us." He was fighting back laughter now, reveling in the success of his capture of Rogue. "She turned a blind eye to our deeds in life. In return, we promised to force any of the men and women we killed to swear undying fealty to the Winter Court. A promise of a life after death, serving under Her Majesty."

Baxter gasped. "You were building an army."

Jennie kept her eyes fixed on the pair. "And after death?"

Eugenio grinned once more, the sight of it predatory.

Jennie likened it to being face to face with a shark.

"A promise of a new life," Eugenio told her. "A deal that my brother and I would be sent across the Atlantic to live our lives as we pleased—under the proviso that we provide a regular supply of specters to the Winter Court, of course."

"I don't understand," Baxter whispered to Jennie, not that it prevented his words from reverberating around an auditorium designed to carry sound. "If the queen had a deal with them, why would she send you to stop them when they were alive?"

Jennie took a calming breath, fighting to maintain her controlled center. "She didn't."

"No, that's right!" Eugenio declared dramatically, standing and pointing his finger at Jennie. "That was an unhappy accident, wasn't it? Another example of how your disobedience of orders and refusing to let go got you into trouble. Queeny didn't want you to pursue us, did she?"

Jennie shrugged. "Nope."

"But you did it anyway, didn't you?" he pressed.

"The hole in your stomach says yes," Jennie replied.

Eugenio looked like he might lose his cool for a moment. "And now here we are, forced to deal with a nuisance who keeps turning up and interfering with things better ignored." The grin returned to his face. "But not for much longer, eh?" He sat next to his brother and waved a hand. "Men. Women. On with the show."

Several dozen guns were cocked at that moment, all of them ready to spray bullets into the mortal and the specter who had gotten in their way. The tension was thick.

"And, *action!*" Carmelo hissed.

Before the first specter fired, the spotlights went out, leaving the theater in darkness.

"What's going on?" Eugenio shouted, his voice laced with rage. "What's happening? Shoot, damn you. *Shoot!*"

The specters fired at the stage. The sound of bullets splintering wood filled the auditorium. After several strobe-like muzzle flashes, it became clear to the group that something was wrong.

Jennie and Baxter were gone.

CHAPTER TWENTY-FOUR

Rico couldn't believe this was happening again.

He hadn't even been invisible. Hadn't even been harnessing his innate spectral gift to disappear completely from sight, yet somehow the bitch had latched onto him and drained his power.

He could see the auditorium around him as though he were driving at warp speed, each individual specter flickering in his line of sight.

Jennie drew closer to him, using his energy to make her and her companion invisible while also pulling the big lummox behind her.

Rico felt paralyzed; his movements weren't his own. He was shocked into stillness by her power as she passed him and gave a cheeky wink, then disappeared behind him with Baxter in tow.

I swear to all the gods, bitch, if you don't release me now, I'll... I'll...

You'll what? Jennie's reply rang in his head. *Send me into the afterlife? Try it. See what happens.*

Rico gulped as Jennie released her connection to him, and found himself slumped on the floor, the stage torn into holes by his comrades' gunfire.

He lay back, only half-hearing the cries of anger from his

bosses. He did, however, clearly hear Jennie utter the single word that would set off the chain reaction for the rest of the fight.

Jennie reappeared behind the row of specters on the stage, her arms in the air as though she were mimicking a bear. "Boo," she called loud enough to startle those around her.

Before the first specter could turn around and point the barrel of his gun at Jennie, she laced her arm through the crook of his and twisted it behind his back.

The gun fell from his hand and she swooped to catch it, ducking just in time to avoid a shot fired at her head.

Baxter slammed the specter with his wrench. He used the momentum to swing his wrench at the person beside him, then quickly maneuvered to take a shot at a guy several feet down the line who held another assault rifle and looked as though he didn't care who he mowed down with it.

I suppose that makes sense. It's not like us specters won't find a way to heal...I hope.

The assault rifle flew out of the specter's hands and over toward the seating.

Jennie, unfazed by the gunfire, managed to block another specter who had decided he would use his handgun to bash her over the head.

She threw her head forward and knocked him into a group of specters about to take a shot.

"Get her, you idiots!" Eugenio raged.

Jennie looked up at the lights and sent another wave of energy toward them. They went out as shots were fired. Cries of pain came from the specters.

Jennie chuckled quietly, already using her mental image of everyone's position to move around in the darkness. She made sure to fire a bullet in Charles' direction before catching two specters by the hair and whacking their heads together, the impact making a satisfying sound like two coconuts colliding.

She jumped to the left, anticipating the charge of a gaunt specter who held a knife.

When she had just about exhausted her memory, she allowed the lights to flash several times like strobe lights.

On the other side of the stage, Baxter held a man's arms behind his back and ran at Rita, using him as a shield.

Rita dived out of the way, her gun falling from her hand as she let out a scream.

All of this happened in a few chaotic seconds that threw the specters into disarray. As each lightning flash occurred, Jennie examined the battlefield to make herself aware of the specters flooding toward the stage from the balconies, the wings, and behind the curtain. They hadn't yet come close to using their full number.

Which was fine by Jennie. She didn't need to take down a hundred specters. She needed to take down two.

She looked at the spot where Eugenio and Carmelo had been sitting and saw that they were on their feet, fear on their faces as they prepared to run. "Hey, arseholes," she called. "Do you want to do this the easy way or the hard way?"

Their pace quickened at the sound of her voice. They ran down the row of seats, stumbling as their feet caught the legs of the chairs.

"Very well." Jennie leveled her pistol. "The hard way, it is."

She lined up the shot and was about to pull the trigger when she heard a shout from behind her. The next thing she knew, she had been wrestled to the floor, and the weight of a specter pinned her to the ground.

She rolled over and felt Worthington's fuzzy bearskin tickling her face.

Jennie shoved her specter off of her. "What are you doing?"

"Saving you from making a huge mistake," Worthington told her.

"They're convicted criminals. Lowlifes. They trafficked women in life, and now they're forcing people to join the paranormal court. Can't you push your loyalties to the queen aside and see that what they're doing is wrong?"

Worthington looked pained. "I'm sorry, Jennie. You've meddled beyond your jurisdiction." He sighed. "This could have been easy."

He rose to his feet and aimed his gun at Jennie's face. Where he had found it, she had no idea.

There was more commotion on the stage as Baxter used the strobing lights to his advantage. He had taken a shot to his wrench arm, but with his stature and strength, he was managing to lift and throw the recovering addicts like they weighed nothing.

"This is easy," Jennie told Worthington. She latched her power onto his and ripped the gun from his hands in one swift motion.

Worthington raised his hands in defense. "You took an oath," A ghostly tear rolled down his cheek. "To obey the crown and Queen Victoria's rule. What right do you have to cause this disruption and upset among the spectral community? It's not your place, Jennie."

"I never took a fucking oath," Jennie snapped, pointing the gun at the center of Worthington's head. "All these years, I've served the queen, believing that what she was doing was right and true. Kicking ass in the name of Her Majesty and ensuring that justice prevailed is my life. Yet, for all those years, she's been subverting her own system and allowing thugs like these shits to help her keep her throne? Where's the justice in that?"

Worthington's mouth dropped open. "You never took an oath?"

Jennie shook her head, aware of the specters around her

motioning to the others to turn their attention to their true enemy. "My loyalties are my own. My only mistress is Justice."

Worthington cried out in alarm as the report rang around the theater. He opened his eyes, surprised to see that Jennie was over the far side of the theater, disappearing in the direction of the Messino brothers.

Baxter jumped off the stage and followed her.

The brothers weren't difficult to find.

Even in death, the brothers were slow. They hadn't taken care of their health in life, and that had translated to their spectral forms. Jennie followed the trail of spectral energy and soon caught up with them in the theater's bar. They were about to disappear through the wall when Jennie closed her eyes and reached out with both her hands and her power to control them.

She channeled her energy the same way she had all those years ago with the little ghost girl at the Savoy, a skill that had grown over the years as she harnessed and refined her power.

Eugenio and Carmelo tried to fight the connection but were dragged back into the room.

Jennie commandeered their spirits and forced them down onto two nearby chairs, where they stared at her with darkness in their eyes.

"You know you can't kill us twice." Eugenio grinned. "To kill a specter? Now, that takes a special kind of gift."

"And think of the queen," Carmelo reminded her. "What will she think when she finds out what you've done?"

Jennie remained silent, considering. Her mind flashed back to the last time she had encountered the brothers and how easy it had been to kill them and free the girls, but they were right. What could she do?

Ordinarily, she would find a way to bind their spirits and

send them to the paranormal court to be tried and serve their sentence. But now, knowing what she knew about the queen, how could she send these men to her?

"Er, Jennie? Not to rush you, but I think we're about to have company."

Jennie strained her ears and heard the excited cries of the specters sprinting through the theater toward them.

Eugenio laughed darkly. "Give up, *Rogue*. You're surrounded."

Jennie waited patiently as the first specters arrived through the walls. The gusto with which they entered the room soon dissipated when they saw their bosses pinned to their chairs. They trained their weapons on Jennie, ready to shoot at the command of the brothers.

The room filled up. Soon there were over sixty specters gathered around Jennie, Eugenio, and Carmelo, yet Jennie held Eugenio's gaze.

Eugenio stared unblinkingly into her eyes. "So, what'll it be? Death, or death?"

Jennie closed her eyes and took a steadying breath. She felt their energy around her as a physical force, a great cloud of power made from the energy of each specter gathered around.

The power hummed inside her. She scanned the specters, searching for the right one to give her what she needed to fix this situation and achieve the desired outcome.

But all she could see were the faces of the addicts. All she could smell was the fetid stench of death from the dressing rooms. As hard as she tried to calm herself, Victoria's face popped into her mind as the source of this injustice—the snake in the grass who had used Jennie's unshaken faith over the years to get her to perform her tasks.

And then the girls. Those sweet girls who deserved nothing more than love from the families they were so crudely torn away from. Prepared to be used and abused because of these two scumbags. How many girls had there been before the ones she'd rescued? How many more would suffer at the hands of the immortal Messino brothers?

Jennie felt the power drawing toward her like some sentient thing. Trails of spectral energy pulled her way as words in Latin came to her mind and began to play on her tongue. Her mouth moved, and she whispered the words of a long-dead language.

"Deus est;

Et inimicos eorum dispersus est

et eos, qui oderunt eum, a facie ejus.

Ut impellere fumum,

pulsi sunt;

liquescit cera a facie ignis

et peccatores coram Deo."

The words grew louder, and the room began to fill with light.

Baxter gasped and tore his eyes away from the ball of light that appeared between Jennie's open palms.

The small sphere grew as the surrounding specters dropped their weapons and clutched their heads, unable to understand what was happening.

Eugenio's voice rang out. "No! What are you doing? Stop. *Stop!"*

Jennie opened her eyes, the pupils completely gone and replaced by holy light. She stared at the orb between her hands, knowing exactly what to do. She continued her chant, reaching a crescendo as she muttered a final, *"Et peccatores coram Deo,"* and hurled the ball of light at the brothers.

The ball smashed into them both and began to spread, morphing into their shapes as though absorbed by their bodies. They exploded in a blinding blast of light.

Then they were gone.

The light faded in less than a second, and their seats were empty.

Silence fell across the room. All specters present stared open-mouthed at the mortal who had just defeated their bosses.

Jennie's mouth was dry, her mind trying to process what just happened. "I thought they could use the exorcise," she muttered.

Baxter snorted awkwardly, unsure whether to laugh, considering they were still surrounded by the enemy.

But the remaining specters made no move to attack. Instead, they remained silent as they backed away and melted into the theater walls.

"That's probably for the best," Jennie conceded, grabbing Baxter by the arm. "Come on, let's find that piece-of-shit Beefeater and see what he has to say for himself."

Neither of them was surprised to find that Worthington had gone, leaving no trace.

CHAPTER TWENTY-FIVE

<u>Midtown Manhattan, New York City, Present Day</u>

"No, no, no. You're doing it all wrong."

Jennie clicked her tongue as she rose from the stool. The bistro was pretty empty at this time of day, the morning light only just beginning to spill in through the window.

She leaped over the counter, pivoted on her hands, and stood by the perplexed barman.

He looked at his colleagues for support, but several of them apparently found the whole thing surprisingly funny. The barman wasn't much more than twenty-one and was relatively new to the role.

He was being shown the ropes by a woman who was over a hundred years his senior.

Not that he would have any idea about that.

"*Fill it* with ice," Jennie instructed, pouring crushed ice into the shaker. "No need to hold back." She measured out a healthy dose of apple brandy and grenadine before grabbing a lemon and squeezing it hard.

Juice sprayed all over the counter, but Jennie didn't mind.

She wouldn't be the one cleaning it up.

She shoved the shaker into the barman's hand. "Now, I imagine you know how to give this a good shake, yes?"

The barman obeyed with a perplexed look on his face. He cautiously began shaking the container by the side of his head. Several waitresses had gathered at the end of the bar and were watching with amusement.

"Good, now pour that into there, and presto!"

The barman obliged and poured a blood-red drink into an angled glass. Jennie garnished the rim with a slice of lemon, sipped from the drink, and smacked her lips.

"Just like my father used to make." She gave the barman a pat on the cheek. "Don't worry, you'll get into your groove soon. Those babies were hot at the beginning of the 1900s. All the rage in early New York."

"You're a historian?" the barman asked, managing to find *some* words at last.

Jennie feigned thinking, touching her finger to her chin. "Of a sort."

She shoved a handful of change into the man's hand and hopped back to the other side of the bar.

Baxter sat on the stool beside her, laughing quietly and shaking his head. "You certainly know how to leave an impression. But did you really have to order a cocktail at…" He looked at the large clock on the wall. "Nine thirty in the morning?"

Jennie shrugged. "Hey, a girl wants what a girl wants."

Baxter grinned.

They sat quietly together for some time, both of them decompressing after the night's events and a less-than-successful hunt for Worthington.

Baxter broke the silence at last. "You're a woman of many talents," he told Jennie, his eyes fixed on two parents wrestling to keep their toddler under control in a far corner of the bistro.

"So I've heard," she replied.

"I've never seen an exorcism performed live before," he

commented, talking almost as if to himself. "I never truly believed I would. How did you do that?"

"I don't know," Jennie answered honestly. "Truth is, there's a lot about my powers that I'll never understand. I try every day to hone them and figure out how I can best use what I've got to help the world. I've tried exorcisms before, but they've never quite worked."

"Maybe you just needed a strong enough reason?" Baxter suggested.

"Or maybe the people I've tried to exorcise have been protected by their oaths to the queen all along." Jennie's eyes narrowed. She still didn't know how to handle the knowledge she'd acquired. To find out that the last hundred or so years had been a lie had shaken her to her core.

Baxter turned when a bell rang and saw a lone woman walk into the bistro. He turned his attention back to Jennie when she sat at the far end of the bar and ordered a drink.

"Your oath..." he started, not entirely sure what to say.

"Yeah," Jennie murmured. "A big surprise, right?"

Baxter nodded.

Jennie took a breath and stared at the wall. A long mirror reflected the necks of the liquor bottles, and she could see herself in it. "The truth is, I've never been under oath. I was indoctrinated into the paranormal court shortly before Victoria took the throne. There was a whole mess with the administration, and in the chaos of kicking William IV off the throne, there was a clerical oversight. No one ever checked my allegiance, and I never thought to mention it again."

Baxter nodded as he absorbed the information. "Yet, you've been serving Victoria ever since?" They each noticed that the other left out the word "Queen" when referring to Victoria, but given the current circumstances, they both understood.

Jennie smiled sadly. "For a hundred and eighteen years. Years after my mentor perished in the great battle of 1902. Years after both my parents perished and passed into the void beyond the veil."

"The great battle of 1902? I didn't know anyone fought before the start of World War I," Baxter admitted. "Who did you fight? Early Nazis? The French?"

"Zombies," Jennie replied straight-faced.

Baxter stared at her a few moments, wondering if she was joking. Her expression did not change.

Jennie raised her drink to her lips and took another deep swallow. Her eyes closed as she inhaled its aroma, and she thought back to the days spent with her father, him making up his own cocktail recipes in the kitchen, experimenting with a thousand different spirits and juices. The "Jack Rose" was his tipple of choice on those end-of-work-week evenings when he could settle in his favorite chair and snuggle with Jennie on his lap.

The memories were brought back by smelling a drink. It seemed somehow impossible, but there it was.

When she opened her eyes, she wasn't surprised to find that the woman who had entered the bistro a few moments ago had migrated to the stool beside her. Her face, bordered with fiery hair and sporting smiling ruby-red lips, sat in the same spot as Baxter, who had his arms held high as if to prove he was innocent.

Jennie grinned. "I was wondering how long it would be before we met again."

Tanya gave her a smile and flicked a lock of hair off her face. "I didn't expect to run into you. This is my morning coffee location." She glanced at Jennie's half-drained drink. "I see you've already gotten the party started."

Jennie raised her glass. "The party never ends."

Tanya giggled, then paused. She clearly wanted to speak but hesitated for some reason.

"What is it?" Jennie asked.

"Well, you made me a promise, remember?"

Jennie did remember. She had made the promise the day she'd confirmed Tanya's suspicions that the spectral world was real, and that life existed beyond death. A promise to introduce Tanya to Worthington.

"There's a slight issue with that, I'm afraid," Jennie apologized. "You see, the specter who accompanied me then has gone AWOL, and I have no idea where to find him."

"Oh." Tanya's head dropped. "What happened?"

Jennie smiled at Baxter. "It's a *long* story. How about we go back to your place, and I'll tell you all about it?"

Tanya agreed, and they headed for the bistro door.

Baxter caught up with them and whispered to Jennie, "What about the queen and the rest of the scum who fled? What about Worthington? Haven't we got things we need to do?"

Jennie waved a hand. "Oh, we'll get to them. Believe it or not, this won't be the first mission I've gone off the books for, and it certainly won't be the last."

"I can believe that." Baxter grinned.

"Who are you talking to?" Tanya asked, her eyes widening with excitement. "Is it *them*? Are they here?"

Jennie laughed, put her hands on Tanya's back, and gently nudged her out the door.

AUTHOR NOTES MICHAEL ANDERLE

Thank you for reading our stories, it means the world to us!

With this series, beginning with *Rogue*, I collaborated to bring a story that somewhat mimicked the history of the United States and England.

Except in the paranormal world, the two countries have never separated.

Rogue is trying to deal with keeping the peace, but the existing power structures are making that harder and harder to accomplish. Read the next set of stories to find out *WHAT HAPPENS NEXT!*

(It will be a total surprise, I promise!)

In the next book, I'm going to introduce Lynne Stiegler from Editor of Editors Inc. (She has a real company name, but this name is much better.)

I bet you she just edited the paragraph above and put in the real company name, didn't you Lynne? (Editor note: I'll just mention it's SkyHunter Partners. But now I'm considering changing it.)

I met Lynne (what seems like a long time ago) via Facebook. She had been sick and so decided to read the Kurtherian Gambit and enjoyed the stories. The editing?

Not so much.

Reaching out, she mentioned her background (editing) and that her husband Marc Stiegler (who I hope will answer these questions in the future) had worked with Baen Books.

A company that has a lot of authors I really enjoy, and she had done editing for them, as well.

One thing led to another, and I asked for some help with our projects. Fortunately for me, Lynne knew her stuff and (almost) anything I threw at her, she caught deftly and made it happen on the editing front. (*Editor's Note: What is this "almost" you speak of Michael? My catcher's mitt is totally worn out!*)

In fact, at the beginning of 2018, I told the company I wanted to accomplish four hundred titles in 2019. By September, she had her team capable of doing 2,000,000 (two million) words of editing per month and those of us responsible for producing 400 titles had no clue what we needed to do yet.

Suffice to say, she and her team made the rest of us scramble ;-)

Stay tuned for more information on Lynne in *Renegade*!

Thank you for spending your time with us!

Ad Aeternitatem,

Michael Anderle

CONNECT WITH THE AUTHOR

Connect with Michael Anderle

Website: http://lmbpn.com

Email List: http://lmbpn.com/email/

Social Media:

https://www.facebook.com/LMBPNPublishing

https://twitter.com/MichaelAnderle

https://www.instagram.com/lmbpn_publishing/

https://www.bookbub.com/authors/michael-anderle